James Rendel Harris

Hermas in Arcadia

And other Essays

James Rendel Harris

Hermas in Arcadia
And other Essays

ISBN/EAN: 9783337397159

Printed in Europe, USA, Canada, Australia, Japan

Cover: Foto ©Andreas Hilbeck / pixelio.de

More available books at **www.hansebooks.com**

HERMAS IN ARCADIA

AND OTHER ESSAYS

BY

J. RENDEL HARRIS, M.A., D.Litt. (Dubl.),

FELLOW OF CLARE COLLEGE, CAMBRIDGE.

CAMBRIDGE:
AT THE UNIVERSITY PRESS.
1896

PREFACE.

IN the following pages I have reprinted two essays which throw
some light on critical problems connected with the text and
interpretation of that famous early Christian book, known as the
Shepherd of Hermas. Each of them has been the starting point
for important investigations by the leading scholars of our time;
and I have endeavoured to indicate the accretions or corrections
which they have made to my first statements, so that the student
may not only have before him the texts of my researches, which
are extant, sometimes in very brief form, in journals not very easy
of access, but may also be able to bring the investigations up to
their latest point of development.

Of these two essays the first appeared in June 1887 in the
Journal of the Society for Biblical Literature and Exegesis
(Boston, U.S.A.); the second is three years earlier in date; it
was first printed in the *Circulars of the Johns Hopkins University*
for April 1884, a publication containing many valuable notes on
all branches of science, but not generally accessible, nor easy to
handle. If the brief paper in question were estimated by the
combat of giants which it provoked, I think it would be admitted
that it was worth reprinting.

To these I have added a number of other pieces which may,
perhaps, be found useful by the critics. Where they do not
permanently instruct, they may transitorily please; and where
the matter of them may seem to be unimportant, the method
will sometimes be found deserving of consideration.

CONTENTS.

THE object of the present paper is to set at rest a critical difficulty which has been raised concerning the interpretation of the tract of Hermas which goes under the heading of the Ninth Similitude; and to indicate a direction in which further light may be obtained on the vexed question of the date of this remarkable writer. The difficulty is in the first instance one of interpretation: we find in the writings of Hermas a blending of the real experiences of life with imaginary importations from current mythologies which render it hard to decide whether the writer wishes us to take him seriously, or to apply to his works an allegorical interpretation such as was common enough in early times, both in pagan and Jewish and Christian circles. And it is probably this perplexity rather than a mere personal fondness for such interpretations which led Origen to explain even the most strongly defined personal allusions in Hermas, the names of Clement and Grapte, in a spiritual manner. We may at least conclude that the subject invited such treatment. We may easily agree that the allusions to his life in Rome in the first Vision are genuine history, from which the step to the second Vision, which contains a visit to Cumæ, seems natural, as does also the account of the walk on the Via Campana in the third Vision. But if we admit these passages to be meant for a literal acceptation, we certainly cannot admit the interview with the Church-Sibyl to be anything but a work of imagination based on popular religious mythology. And we should not find it easy to determine where the literal ends and the allegorical begins. We are thus in much the same case as an interpreter of the Pilgrim's Progress would be who had sufficient knowledge of Bunyan's history to see that the "certain den" with which the book opens is the Bedford prison, and who had sufficient

insight to determine that the rest of the book was allegorical, but
who was wanting both in the historical information and in the
intuitive perception by which to detect the traces of Bunyan's
personal history which lurk behind the folds of the Allegory. It
is however generally held that the mention of places not very
remote from Rome ought to be accepted as sufficient evidence that
the writer is giving us history rather than romance. The Via
Campana, at least, scarcely admits of being allegorized, nor the
mile-stones which Hermas passes on the road: with Cumæ the
question is a little more involved, but even here the general
opinion has been, and probably will remain in favour of the positive
geographical acceptation of Hermas' words.

Such being the case, it is not a little surprising that, when we
have so many Italian allusions in the book of Visions, we should
find ourselves transported in the Ninth Similitude into Arcadia,
and there regaled with an allegorical account of the building of
the Church, which outdoes in fantastic detail the whole of the
previous accounts. Are we to assume that, as in the case quoted
from the Pilgrim's Progress, the initial note of place is to be
accepted literally, and that from that point we plunge into
allegory; or is the whole a work of imagination from the start?
In the latter case, how can we explain the change of literary
method involved in the comparison between a real Rome, Cumæ,
Via Campana, and a poetic Arcadia? In the former case, how did
the Roman Hermas find his way into the most inaccessible part of
Greece? It was no doubt through some such questioning that
Zahn was led to propose an emendation in the text of Hermas so
that instead of reading

$$\text{καὶ ἀπήγαγέν με εἰς 'Αρκαδίαν}$$

we should put 'Αρικίαν for 'Αρκαδίαν. The advantage of this
correction was that it transferred the scene again to the neighbourhood of Rome, and restored the literary parallelism between the
Ninth Similitude and the book of Visions. To support this
conjecture, Zahn first brought forward a case where the word
'Αρικίαν had been corrupted in transcription, viz.: a passage in
the Acts of Peter and Paul, c. 20, where the scribe has in error
given 'Αραβίαν. If Arabia, why not Arcadia?

Then he proceeds to shew that the country around Aricia
corresponds to the description given by Hermas of Arcadian

scenery, and, in particular, he identifies the "rounded hill" (ὅρος μαστῶδες) to which Hermas was transported, with the Italian *Monte Gentile.* I do not know whether this suggestion of Zahn has met with any great favour, although it is ingenious, and not outside the bounds of possibility. The objection to it is chiefly that which falls to the lot of the majority of conjectural emendations, viz.: that it is not necessary; for, as I shall shew presently, the whole description of the country visited by Hermas, corresponds closely with the current accounts of Arcadian scenery, and is probably based upon them. So that if I do not discuss Zahn's hypothesis directly, it is because it is a last resort of criticism to which one must not look until the normal methods of interpretation have broken down. Let us then examine the scene into which Hermas introduces us; and the interpretation which he puts upon what he sees. We are told in the first place that his guide led him away into Arcadia and there seated him upon the top of a rounded hill from whence he had a view of a wide plain surrounded by mountains of diverse character and appearance. We will indicate the description of these mountains by the following diagram, in which the successive eminences are ranged in a circular form, and attached to each is the leading characteristic which is noted by Hermas:—

<table>
<tr><td></td><td></td><td>ζ
×</td><td></td><td></td></tr>
<tr><td>πηγῶν πλήρες</td><td>η'×</td><td>εἶχε
βοτάνας ἱλαρὰς
καὶ πᾶν γένος
κτηνῶν καὶ ὀρνέων</td><td>×ς'</td><td>σχισμῶν ὅλον ἔγεμεν
.. εἶχον δὲ βοτάνας αἱ
σχισμαί</td></tr>
<tr><td>θ'×
ὅλον ἐρημῶδες
.. ἕρπετα θανατώδη</td><td></td><td></td><td>×ε'</td><td>ἔχον βοτάνας
χλωρὰς καὶ
τραχὺ ὄν</td></tr>
<tr><td>εἶχε δένδρα μέγιστα ι'×
... καὶ πρόβατα</td><td></td><td>×
ὄρος μαστῶδες</td><td>×δ'</td><td>βοτάνας ἔχον·
ἡμιξήρους</td></tr>
<tr><td>δένδρα κατάκαρπα ια'×</td><td></td><td></td><td>×γ'</td><td>ἀκανθῶν καὶ
τριβόλων πλῆρες</td></tr>
<tr><td>ὅλον λευκόν ιβ'×</td><td></td><td>×
α'
μέλαν ὡς ἀσβόλη</td><td>×β'</td><td>ψιλόν, βοτάνας μὴ ἔχον</td></tr>
</table>

Now before we begin to look for identifications with the scenery of any particular country or neighbourhood, we should try to subtract from the description those details which are artistically inserted by Hermas in order to bring certain views of his own before the minds of his reader under the cover of his allegory. The matter of the Ninth Similitude so far as it concerns the building of the tower and the shaping of the various stones is already present in the third Vision; and there is much in the description that is parallel to the account given of the various stones which are brought from the twelve mountains. For example, just as in the third Vision we find stones brought for building that are white, and some that are speckled (ἐψωριακότες); some that are squared, and some that are round; some that are sound, and some that have cracks in them. When we find, therefore, that in his Ninth Similitude Hermas makes his first mountain black as soot and his twelfth perfectly white, we know that it is more likely to be an expansion of the previous allegory than a natural feature; and when we find him saying that some of the mountains had chasms (σχισμαί) in them, we must rather refer to the stones that have cracks in them (σχισμὰς ἔχοντες) than to any peculiarity of the mountain region, however the description may seem to invite the identification with the peculiar characteristic of Arcadia, the κατάβαθρα or underground passages and hollows of the mountains into which the rivers of that country so commonly precipitate themselves.

A similar process of subtraction must be made on account of the similarity between this Ninth Similitude and the one that precedes it. In this case the allegory turns upon the distribution by the angel of the Lord of a number of branches which he had cut from a great willow-tree. After a while the angel summons the people to whom he had given them and scrutinizes them carefully. Some brought back their branches withered, others half-withered and with cracks on their surface, (ἡμιξήρους καὶ σχισμὰς ἐχούσας,) others again were green, (χλωράς,) others had fruit, and so on. A comparison of these terms with those used by Hermas of his mountains will shew that there has been a use made of the Eighth Similitude in the Ninth.

Nor must we suppose that there is any special identification with the particular number twelve. The number is introduced artificially and for the following reason: the mountains out of which the stones are taken are declared to represent the peoples of the earth out of whom the church is builded; now the idea prevailed at an early period that since the Jewish Ecclesia was composed of twelve tribes, something of a similar nature was to be predicated concerning the Christian world which had replaced and comprehended the Jewish world. Otherwise how was an explanation possible of the sealing of the 144,000 in the Apocalypse? But then these twelve tribes could not be identified with nationalities and must therefore represent so many different types of character.

This is undoubtedly Hermas' idea, and it shews us that we must not suppose any geographical enumeration to be involved in the number twelve. The author of the *Opus Imperfectum in Matthaeum* amongst his many traces of antiquity gives us the following on Matt. xix. 28: "Adhuc autem audeo, et subtiliorem introducere sensum, et sententiam alterius cuiusdam viri referre. Exponit autem sic: Quoniam sicut Judaeorum populus in duodecim tribus fuit divisus, sic et universus populus Christianus divisus est in duodecim tribus secundum quasdam proprietates animorum et diversitates cordium, quas solus deus discernere et cognoscere potest, ut quaedam animae sunt de tribu Reuben, quaedam de tribu Simeon vel Levi vel Juda."

These twelve classes according to Hermas are

α. Blasphemers and traitors.

β. Hypocrites and wicked teachers.

γ. Rich men and those who are involved in the business of life[1].

δ. The double-minded.

ε. Badly-trained, self-willed people.

ϛ. Slanderers and keepers of grudges.

ζ. Simple, guileless, happy souls who give of their toils without hesitating and without reproach. (Cf. Teaching of Apostles.)

η. Apostles and teachers.

θ. Bad deacons who have plundered the widow and orphan. Lapsi who do not repent and return to the saints.

---

[1] Note that these are said to be πνιγόμενοι ὑπὸ τῶν πράξεων αὐτῶν, and correspond to the mountain covered with thorns and briars; the reference to the Gospel (the thorns sprang up and choked them) seems indisputable.

ι. Hospitable bishops who entertain the servants of God.

ια. Martyrs for the Name, including those who thereby obtain a remission that was otherwise inaccessible to them.

ιβ. Babes of the Kingdom who keep all the commands of God.

These, then, are the twelve tribes of the new Israel; and, as I have said, we do need to identify twelve mountains.

When we have made the deductions intimated from the imagery, we are left to identify the locality from the remaining data; and this we shall proceed to do. And to begin with, let us observe that the idea of Arcadia presented itself early in connection with Christianity. For example, that beautiful composition which passes under the name of the second epistle of Clement, but which seems rather to be an early Christian homily, declares (c. xiv) the pre-existence of the Church in the following terms: "Wherefore, my brethren, if we do the will of God our Father we shall be of the first Church, viz.: the spiritual one, which *was created before the sun and moon*... For the Church was spiritual as was also our Jesus[1], and was manifested in the last times." No doubt this language is in part to be explained like the Valentinian Syzygy of Man and the Church by reference to a gnosis on Genesis i. 27. The writer of the homily says as much; the first Adam having been created male with female, so was the second; but what should be noticed is that the terms used to describe the pre-existence are not borrowed from Genesis, but from the Arcadian tradition that they existed in their mountain fastnesses before the moon, and it was thus that they explained their name of Προσέληνοι. What the writer of the homily means is that the Christian Church is the true Arcadia. And thus we have at once the explanation of the ideal journey which Hermas makes into Arcadia. For we find the same view held in the second Vision of Hermas (Vis. ii. 4. 1), where we are told even more decidedly that the Church was created first of all things. Similar ideas must have been common enough in the earlier centuries. So much being premised, let us put ourselves into the position of Hermas on the supposition that he has no more than the ordinary notions concerning Arcadia. We should simply be

---

[1] That Christ was before "the Sun and Moon" is proved by Justin, *Dial.* 76, apparently from Ps. 72. 17, 110. 3.

able to say that Arcadia was the innermost part of the Peloponnesus, and that it was shut in on every side by a ring of mountains. The rudest idea that could be formed would therefore be that of a plain within a circular mountain-wall; precisely the kind of view with which the Ninth Similitude opens. Here dwell the remnants of the primitive and virtuous race of men whom the gods loved to visit, whose chief virtues were, according to Polybius, φιλοξενία and φιλανθρωπία. It may be noticed in passing, though I do not attach any importance to it, that Hermas makes one of his spiritual tribes, the good bishops, representative of the virtue of hospitality.

But it is plain that Hermas' knowledge goes beyond the elementary notion sketched above. This can be seen best by noticing the points which occur in the description of the mountains which have no special parallel in the allegorical explanation of the characters whom the mountains represent. For example, he adds to his description of his seventh mountain the fact that there were found on it all manner of beasts and birds; the eighth mountain is full of springs; the tenth mountain has sheep resting under the shade of its timber; the ninth is full of snakes and evil beasts; the eleventh shews fruit trees, and so on. But especially one should draw attention to the sixth mountain, whose description is ἔχον βοτάνας χλωρὰς καὶ τραχὺ ὄν. The same language is used again in c. 22 τοῦ ἔχοντος βοτάνας χλωρὰς καὶ τραχέος ὄντος. Here all the editors print the word τραχύ as an adjective, and it may be so; but if an adjective it is suggested by the name of one of the mountains of Arcadia. A reference to a map of Arcadia will shew this mountain on the eastern side of the plain of Orchomenos: E. Curtius in his Peloponnesos (i. 219) describes it as follows: "Den östlichen Berg nannten die Alten seiner rauhen und schroffen Form wegen Trachy."

I suppose it will hardly be maintained to be an accidental coincidence that Hermas, writing of Arcadia, or professing to do so, should twice describe a particular mountain by the name which the ancients used to designate one of the mountains of Arcadia. So far from any such assumption being likely, the mere mention of the name Trachy would be sufficient to intimate that we were in Arcadia.

This identification being then made, we are able to take the next step, and to determine the plain in which the scene is laid and the rounded hill from which the scenery is viewed. This seems at first sight to be difficult, because, although to an outsider Arcadia might be pictured as a happy valley within mountains, in reality, like Switzerland, with which it has often been compared, it does not furnish any one central plain, but innumerable valleys and small plains; and although there are one or two larger and more spacious than others, none seems to correspond to the rounded form which Hermas' language would at first lead us to expect. But the mention of Mount Trachy shews that the plain must be the plain of Orchomenos, in the midst of which stands, dividing it into upper and lower respectively, the hill of Orchomenos, the strongest natural fortress of Arcadia and perhaps of ancient Greece. This then must be the ὄρος μαστῶδες of Hermas; it rises to a height of nearly 3000 feet immediately from the plain, and was famous even in Homeric times as one of the early Greek strongholds and cities[1].

Thus far we might have arrived from a study of the itinerary of Pausanias, from whose description of Arcadia we must make not a few references. Thus in xiii. § 2 we have the following notes: Ὀρχομενίοις δὲ ἡ προτέρα πόλις ἐπὶ ὄρους ἦν ἄκρᾳ τῇ κορυφῇ καὶ ἀγορᾶς τε καὶ τειχῶν ἐρείπια λείπεται: and in § 3. ἔστι δὲ ἀπαντικρὺ τῆς πόλεως ὄρος Τραχύ. τὸ δὲ ὕδωρ τὸ ἐκ τοῦ θεοῦ διὰ χαράδρας ῥέον κοίλης μεταξὺ τῆς τε πόλεως καὶ τοῦ Τραχέος ὄρους κάτεισιν ἐς ἄλλο Ὀρχομένιον πεδίον· τὸ δὲ πεδίον τοῦτο μεγέθει μὲν μέγα, τὰ πλείω δέ ἐστιν αὐτοῦ λίμνη. It appears, therefore, that the name Trachy was current for the mountain on the east of Orchomenos in the second century: Pausanias seems to have given us here a careful and correct description of the country.

Some of the other mountains to which Hermas makes reference may now be identified by the aid of Pausanias. For example, the ninth mountain is said to be full of serpents and noxious beasts. The mountain referred to is Mt. Sepia. The name is supposed to be derived from the venomous viper that was found there; and there were legends enough about the neighbourhood, even in Pausanias' time, to make it appear a country which was formerly something like Ireland before the arrival of St. Patrick.

[1] Curtius, *Peloponnesos*, i. 220. "Die orchomenische Berg, eine Kuppe von 2912 F. Höhe, welche Ithome ähnlich ist, und wie diese zwei Ebenen beherrscht, steigt unmittelbar aus dem Nachlande empor."

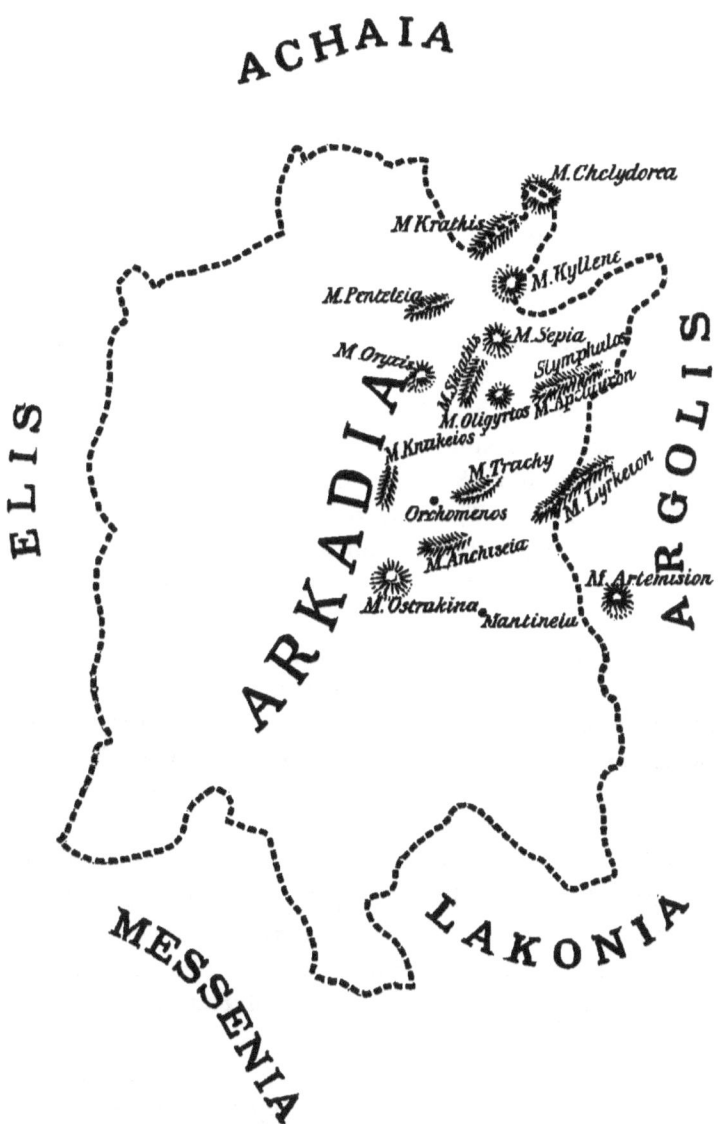

MAP ILLUSTRATING HERMAS' VISIT TO ARCADIA

Here they said that Æpytus, the son of Elatos, met his death from the bite of a serpent. Cf. Pausan. *Arcad.* iv. 4, Κλείτορι δὲ τῷ 'Αζᾶνος οὐ γενομένων παίδων ἐς Αἴπυτον 'Ελάτου περιεχώρησεν ἡ 'Αρκάδων βασιλεία. τὸν δὲ Αἴπυτον ἐξελθόντα ἐς ἄγραν θηρίων μὲν τῶν ἀλκιμωτέρων οὐδὲν, σὴψ δὲ οὐ προϊδόμενον ἀποκτίννυσι. τὸν δὲ ὄφιν τοῦτον καὶ αὐτός ποτε εἶδον· κατὰ ἔχιν ἐστὶ τὸν μικρότατον, τέφρᾳ ἐμφερής, στίγμασιν οὐ συνέχεσι πεποικιλμένος κτέ. xvi. 1, Τρικρήνων δὲ οὐ πόρρω ἄλλο ἐστὶν ὄρος Σηπία καὶ Αἰπύτῳ τῷ 'Ελάτου λέγουσιν ἐνταῦθα γενέσθαι τὴν τελευτὴν ἐκ τοῦ ὄφεως κτέ.

Now, I think, if we compare Pausanias' account of Æpytus' death while hunting, through no great beast, but by the bite of a viper, with Hermas' statement that in the ninth mountain there were ἕρπετα θανατώδη, διαφθείροντα τοὺς ἀνθρώπους, he will have little doubt that the mountain meant is Mt. Sepia.

The identification of these two mountains, Trachy and Sepia, I regard as established. They are respectively the fifth and ninth of Hermas' series, and whatever further progress in identification is possible, the results must harmonize with these so that the other mountains enclose a plain with them, and from an examination of the situation of these two on a map of Arcadia it is not difficult to infer that the order in which Hermas reckons his mountains is East—North—West—South. I am not, however, very sanguine of making any further identifications that would be equally convincing. It would be, however, possible to detect the origin of Hermas' many-fountained mountain. For we are informed by Pausanias that the emperor Adrian brought water for the city of Corinth all the way from Stymphalus: Paus. ii. iii. 5, Κρῆναι δὲ πολλαὶ μὲν ἀνὰ τὴν πόλιν πεποίηνται πᾶσαι, ἅτε ἀφθόνου ῥέοντός σφισιν ὕδατος, καὶ ὃ δὴ βασιλεὺς 'Αδριανὸς ἐσήγαγεν ἐκ Στυμφήλου. The language of Pausanias is in close correspondence with Hermas, and the mountain is located in the eighth place in the field of view. The umbrageous mountain under the shade of which flocks of sheep were gathered might find its identification in the Mt. Skiathis, described by Pausanias as follows, xiv. 1, Καρνῶν δὲ στάδια πέντε ἀφέστηκεν ἥ τε "Ορυξις καλουμένη καὶ ἕτερον Σκίαθις. ὑφ' ἑκατέρῳ δὲ ἔστι τῷ ὄρει βάραθρον τὸ ὕδωρ καταδεχόμενον τὸ ἐκ·τοῦ πεδίου.

According to this identification Mt. Skiathis should be the next in order to Mt. Sepia, since it is the tenth on Hermas' circle; and a reference to the map will shew that this conclusion is not contradicted by the geography of the region, except that I think Skiathis would appear a little to the right of Mt. Sepia to an observer on the hill of Orchomenos[1]. As to the other character-istics, it is not worth while to discuss the animal and vegetable products of Arcadia more at length: it is sufficient to say that Hermas' description shews a very fair acquaintance with ancient Greek geography: and we may naturally go on to enquire what were the sources of his knowledge.

I think that it will be sufficiently evident from what has gone before that there is at least a suspicion that the description is taken from Pausanias. When we remove from our minds those details which I have shewn to be artificial creations of Hermas, and such generalities as attach themselves naturally to the idea of Arcadia as seen from the outside, we are left with peculiarities that at once fall in with the notes in the Itinerary of Pausanias. And these peculiarities are not the striking features of the Arcadian scenery, such as the lofty Mt. Cyllene[2] and the like, but somewhat insignificant details which would hardly have been noted except by a close observer who was making his own notes carefully as he went along, nor would they have been repeated except by some one who had carefully perused such an itinerary[3].

Now here a difficulty presents itself. No doubt we may admit a certain amount of agreement between Pausanias and Hermas, and it would be strange if two second-century writers, both dealing with the subject of Arcadia, had not expressed themselves in a

---

[1] Note that Curtius says (i. 210), "Σκίαθις ist der schattige Waldberg, gleich σύσκιον ὄρος bei Dikaearch. 75. Diesem Bergnamen entspricht der Name des Dorfes Skotini das am Abhange unseres Skiathis liegt."

[2] We cannot even be sure whether Hermas alludes to Mt. Cyllene at all; yet it must have been the most conspicuous feature of the landscape. The fact that it is not actually on the borders of the plain of Orchomenos, proves nothing; Mt. Sepia overlooks the valley of Stymphalus rather than the plain of Orchomenos, yet it is clearly alluded to by Hermas. Is Mt. Cyllene intended by the seventh mountain upon whose slopes are found all kinds of cattle and of birds?

[3] For example, in addition to what has been said, notice that the leading feature in the southwest of the landscape is Mt. Ostrakina, and compare the description in Hermas where the pastor bids those who build the tower to bring ὄστρακον and ἀσβεστος in order that they may make the neighbourhood of the tower clean against the day of its inspection: ὕπαγε καὶ φέρε ἀσβεστον καὶ ἄστρακον λεπτόν. Is this Ostrakina the twelfth mountain of Hermas?

manner which suggested peculiar coincidences in minor points,
but in that case how could it be possible that Hermas could have
utilized Pausanias, when that writer had not completed his Arcadia
before the year 167 (as we shall shew)?

For determining the date of Pausanias' Itinerary we have, I
believe, no facts besides those which are contained in the work
itself. The chronological landmarks are as follows: In the seventh
book of the Itinerary (Achaia 20, § 6) Pausanias explains that the
Odeion at Athens was not described in his first book on Attica
because Herodes Atticus had not built it at the time when the
first book was written. Now Atticus is one of the leading figures
of the second century, sufficiently known by his reputation as a
rhetorician, an executor of magnificent public works all over
Greece, and as a teacher and friend of Marcus Aurelius. The
period of his life is supposed to be A.D. 104–180. Since the close
of his life was embittered by the plots and complaints of an
opposing faction at Athens, we may suspect that his liberality in
public building at Athens does not belong to the last years of his
life. And, whatever date we may assign to the structure, we
have the following sequence :—

> Pausanias writes his Attica.
> Herodes builds the Odeion.
> Pausanias writes his Arcadia.

The other landmark is as follows: Pausanias alludes in his Itinerary
of Arcadia to Marcus Aurelius and, perhaps, to his victory over the
Quadi which took place in A.D. 174. The passage is as follows:
Τοῦτον Εὐσεβῆ τὸν βασιλέα ἐκάλεσαν οἱ Ῥωμαῖοι, διότι τῇ ἐς τὸ
δεῖον τιμῇ μάλιστα ἐφαίνετο χρώμενος· δόξῃ δὲ ἐμῇ καὶ τὸ ὄνομα
τὸ Κύρου φέροιτο ἂν τοῦ πρεσβυτέρου, πατὴρ ἀνθρώπων καλού-
μενος. Ἀπέλιπε δὲ καὶ ἐπὶ τῇ βασιλείᾳ παῖδα ὁμώνυμον· ὁ δὲ
Ἀντωνῖνος οὗτος ὁ δεύτερος καὶ τούς τε Γερμάνους, μαχιμωτάτους
καὶ πλείστους τῶν ἐν τῇ Εὐρώπῃ βαρβάρων καὶ ἔθνος τὸ Σαυρο-
μάτων πολέμου καὶ ἀδικίας ἄρξαντας τιμωρούμενος ἐπεξῆλθε.

The language here used has generally been taken to mean
that Pausanias was writing his eighth book subsequently to the
defeat of the Quadi in 174. But it seems to me that while the
passage has an air of having brought recent history down to date,
that date is the date of the departure of the expedition against
the Germans and not of its return. It becomes therefore possible

to push back the date of the Arcadia nearly seven years earlier. We proceed on the supposition that Pausanias wrote his history and published it as he went along; this appears from the fact that the eighth book was written at a time when the first book was out of reach of correction. But even, on the earliest hypothesis, does it seem likely that Hermas could have written so late in the second century as to copy Pausanias? And if this seem too difficult an assumption, especially in view of the Muratorian canon, is there any other hypothesis that will explain the apparent coincidence? The alternative that first offers itself is the depression of the date of this portion of Hermas.

It has been noticed by Hilgenfeld that the writings attributed to Hermas fall, upon critical examination, into three groups: the first of these which Hilgenfeld calls *Hermas apocalypticus*, comprises the first four Visions; the second part, which comprises Vis. v to Sim. vii, having Vis. iii for its prologue, and Similitude vii for its epilogue, is the true *Hermas pastoralis* or book of the Shepherd. The third division comprises Similitudes viii and ix with the tenth for an epilogue. This part of the book Hilgenfeld calls *Hermas secundarius*, and attributes to his editorial care (whoever he may be) the massing together of the whole series of writings. Now there is something to be said for this division, even if we may not feel like abandoning altogether the theory of the single authorship. May it not be that the last division is the later workmanship of the same hand as wrote the two former groups? In that case we are able still to hold to the Muratorian statement with the single restriction that it applies only to the earlier parts of the book. This would require us to assume that Hermas outlived his brother Pius by a number of years, depending, in part, upon the (doubtful) date of the death of Pius, or at least of the close of his episcopate. And even if this explanation be considered insufficient, it is still possible to adopt Hilgenfeld's theory of a later writer who re-edits and makes an appendix to the earlier Hermas (I do not of course mean to imply that Hilgenfeld makes Hermas fall so late as my theory would imply). And even if Pausanias should turn out not to be the true authority, the identification of the water sources of Corinth brought by Hadrian remains and lowers the date of Hermas accordingly.

It becomes proper now to return to the Arcadian allegory and see whether there is any other point where the comparison can be made geographically correct. And I should like, though in a somewhat tentative manner, to suggest that in the details of the building of the tower, Hermas has had some reference to the early Cyclopean buildings of which the ruins were still to be seen in Greece and especially in the Peloponnesus. Perhaps the best way to make my meaning clear will be to compare a passage in Hermas with descriptions taken from Pausanias and modern writers. In Sim. ix. vii. 4, we find Hermas speaking as follows: "I said to the Shepherd, How can these stones which have been condemned enter into the building of the tower? He answered and said unto me, Dost thou see these stones? I see them, sir, said I. Said he, I will cut away the greater part of these stones and put them into the building, and they shall fit in with the rest of the stones. How, sir, said I, can these stones when cut occupy the same room? He answered and said unto me, Those which are found to be small for their place shall be put into the middle of the building, while the larger ones shall be put outside, and so they will hold one another together."

Now let us compare with this the description which Pausanias gives of the wonderful Cyclopean walls of Tiryns. He tells us that these walls are made of unwrought stones of such size that a team of mules would not be able to shake even the smallest ones; and that smaller stones to these are fitted into the interstices of the larger ones, so as to produce the closest union between them[1].

I understand Hermas to mean to describe in his builded tower a work of Cyclopean character (which, by the way, appears also from the fact that there are only ten stones in the first course of the building), and the small stones which result from the process of cutting, to correspond to those which Pausanias describes as producing a union between the larger blocks. And it is clear from the description in Hermas that the larger blocks are un-wrought stones (ἀργά). Those who wish to see the appearance of such a wall depicted will find it in Schliemann, *Mycenæ and Tiryns*, p. 29, where it is called a "wall of the first period."

Similar Cyclopean remains may be found at other points in

---

[1] τὸ δὴ τεῖχος, ὃ δὴ μόνον τῶν ἐρειπίων λείπεται, κυκλώπων μέν ἐστιν ἔργον, πεποίηται δὲ ἀργῶν λίθων, μέγεθος ἔχων ἕκαστος λίθος ὡς ἀπ' αὐτῶν μηδ' ἂν ἀρχὴν κινηθῆναι τὸν μικρότατον ὑπὸ ζεύγους ἡμιόνων· λίθια δὲ ἐνήρμοσται πάλαι ὡς αὐτῶν ἕκαστον ἁρμονίαν τοῖς μεγάλοις λίθοις εἶναι. Paus. ii. 25, 8.

the Peloponnesus, such as the top of the mountain of Orchómenos, and the ruins of the ancient city of Lycosura in Southwest Arcadia.

And this identification helps us to explain a detail in Hermas' account; viz.: the way in which his tower is said to be built over the rock and *over the gate* (ἐπάνω τῆς πέτρας καὶ ἐπάνω τῆς πύλης). Special attention is given in these early buildings, such as the acropolis of Mycenæ and the like, to the defences of the entrance. The entrance to the gate of the Lions at Mycenæ is an illustration of this, the gate being placed at right angles to the wall of the citadel and approached through a passage formed by the citadel wall and a nearly parallel outer wall which formed part of the masonry of a tower by which the entrance was guarded. Schliemann adds to his description of this gateway an approving reference to Leake for pointing out that "the early citadel builders bestowed greater labour than their successors on the approaches to the gates." Another instance of a gate defended by a tower which projects over it is given by Curtius from the ruins of Lycosura: "On the east side of the city there is preserved a gate with a projecting tower (ein Thor mit einem Thurmvorsprunge)."

I venture the suggestion, then, that Hermas in the Ninth Similitude, when working up again the subject of the Church-Tower, has been influenced by accounts of the Cyclopean buildings of the Peloponnesus. If his authority was a written one, it may have been Pausanias, as in the previous cases; unless some point can be brought forward to show that Pausanias was unacquainted with what Hermas describes elsewhere, and that Hermas must have had written authority for the same.

To sum up the whole course of the preceding arguments: the scene of the Ninth Similitude of Hermas is really laid in Arcadia, probably in the plain of Orchomenos. Some of the mountain scenery which he describes is capable of exact identification by means of the Itinerary of Pausanias; and he has been influenced in his architecture by the Cyclopean remains of the Peloponnesus. Either the whole or at all events the latter part of the writings of Hermas should therefore be held of later date than the Arcadia of Pausanias. But the objection will be made that recent researches of German investigators and archæologists have shown reason for believing Pausanias himself to be a wholesale thief and plunderer

of previous guide-books to Greece. So that our investigation may
lead rather to the reopening of the Pausanias question than to
the solution of the Hermas chronology and geography.

The attack upon Pausanias was commenced by Wilamowitz-
Möllendorf (*Hermes* xii. 72) and sharply reinforced by Hirschfeld
in an article in the *Archäologische Zeitung* (XL = 1882, f. 97).
Hirschfeld brings a good deal of evidence to shew that the list of
statues of Olympian victors does not reach later than the second
century B.C.; and that the series stops here, not because there
were no more Olympian victories commemorated, but because .
Pausanias is copying an earlier writer (probably Polemo), who
does not pass this point of time in his descriptions: so that we
may almost say that there is no evidence that Pausanias ever
visited Olympia at all; but that both he and Pliny drew upon
earlier writers.

Now this problem is a very many-sided one, and the archæo-
logical world is still divided over it, and, until the discussion
subsides somewhat, it is not easy to determine whether the
defenders of Pausanias or his severe critics have won the day.
My own judgment is still reserved upon the point. Hence we
must also be careful in reference to Hermas. We may be reasonably sure that if Pausanias was never at Olympia, he was never in
Arcadia; but the preliminary hypothesis is not yet settled.
Hence we content ourselves in the Hermas problem with affirm-
ing that Hermas really describes Arcadian scenery, but whether
he takes his description from Pausanias or from some earlier
Baedeker's Guide to Arcadia is as yet uncertain.

After the appearance of the foregoing paper, I received the following remarks upon it from Dr Hort, the characteristic caution of which will be evident to the reader, as I hope it will also be evident presently that the caution was undue and unnecessary.

CAMBRIDGE,
23 Dec. 1887.

..... The first reading interested me much, but not with conviction; for the time, at least, the coincidences seemed too slight. The passage from *Op. Imperf.* at p. 73, a book which has much from Origen, is probably founded on some lost passage of him. There is a reference, though in somewhat ambiguous terms in the *Comm. in Matt.* p. 688 Ru. (1325 A, Migne); cf. 480 (912 A) .....

Dr Lightfoot was more favourable in his view of the argument, but he demurred (as we shall see, rightly) to the assumption that Hermas was indebted to Pausanias.

He wrote as follows:

AUCKLAND CASTLE, BISHOP AUCKLAND,
Nov. 14, 1887.

MY DEAR SIR,

I am much obliged to you for your very interesting paper on *Hermas in Arcadia.*

You seem to me to make out a very strong case for Arcadia. As for Pausanias, I am less able to follow you. But you do not insist on this, nor does it affect your main point. If his information had been derived from Pausanias, I should have expected to find the resemblances go much further.

Yours very sincerely,

J. B. DUNELM.

At this point the argument was taken up by Mr (now Prof.) Armitage Robinson, who published, in an Appendix to his edition of Lambros' collation of the Athos Codex of the Shepherd of

Hermas, some further considerations, which will be found sufficient to dissipate the suspicions aroused by Dr Hort, and to confirm those expressed by Dr Lightfoot.

Over and above the identifications which I had suggested between the Arcadian mountains and the scenery described by Hermas, Mr Robinson suggested four further positive identifications as well as some of a more shadowy character. These are as follows:

(i) Mt Knakalus described by Pausanias (viii. 23. 3, 4); κνᾶκος is the Doric form of κνῆκος a kind of thistle, and consequently this mountain is to be equated with the mountain which Hermas describes as ἀκανθῶδες καὶ τριβόλων πλῆρες (Sim. ix. 1. 5).

(ii) A ridge close to Mt Sepia, called Τρίκρηνα. 'This no doubt was an abbreviation of Τρικάρηνα, the three-peaked ridge; but its popular explanation is all that we have to do with, and that is shewn by the legend that is attached to it: ὄρη Φενεατῶν ἐστὶ Τρίκρηνα καλούμενα· καὶ εἰσὶν αὐτόθι κρῆναι τρεῖς· ἐν ταύταις λοῦσαι τεχθέντα Ἑρμῆν αἱ περὶ τὸ ὄρος λέγονται νύμφαι, καὶ ἐπὶ τούτῳ τὰς πηγὰς ἱερὰς Ἑρμοῦ νομίζουσιν' (Paus. viii. 16. 1).

Accordingly Mr Robinson identified this with the mountain which Hermas describes as πηγῶν πλῆρες...καὶ πᾶν γένος τῆς κτίσεως τοῦ κυρίου ἐποτίζοντο ἐκ τῶν πηγῶν τοῦ ὄρους ἐκείνου.

The next two identifications are less satisfactory:

(iii) A mountain is mentioned by Pausanias, called Phalanthus, and since φάλανθος is synonymous with φαλακρὸς which, like ψιλὸς, means 'bald,' Mr Robinson proposed to identify this with a mountain which Hermas describes as ψιλὸν, βοτάνας μὴ ἔχον. This seems to me too artificial; if Hermas had been describing this mountain, it is much more likely that he would have preserved its Greek name, in the same way as he preserved the name of Τραχύ.

(iv) The next identification I am almost ashamed to cast a suspicion upon. Mr Robinson replied to my question as to the omission of Mt Kyllene from the panorama of Hermas, when it must have been the most conspicuous feature in the landscape, by suggesting that Mt Kyllene is the twelfth mountain of Hermas, the great white, glad-faced mountain, 'unreached by either cloud or wind, so that the very ashes on the altar of Hermes were found undisturbed whenever the worshippers returned for the annual sacrifice.'

There is no doubt that this profound calm of the mountain of Hermes was a favourite thought with the ancients; it has survived for us in modern poetry in the beautiful lines of Wordsworth, where he praises

> .... the perpetual warbling that prevails
> In Arcady, beneath unaltered skies,
> Through the long year in constant quiet bound,
> Night hushed as night, and day serene as day.
>
> *Excursion,* Bk. iii.

Unfortunately, however, and this is the only serious objection to the identification, the mountain Kyllene is, as Mr Robinson knows from an actual visit to the spot, invisible from the hill of Orchomenos; and it seems unlikely that Hermas would have thrust into his panorama a mountain which did not properly form a part of it. He might, perhaps, have done so, if he had been simply working from a geography or a guide-book; but the result of Mr Robinson's additions to my identifications is such as to make it impossible for me to hold any longer the theory of borrowing from Pausanias. Hermas must have been in Arcadia, and in that case, it is very unlikely that he would have given us an incorrect landscape. I will not say it is impossible, and I should be glad if further consideration should make it appear more probable.

But enough has been said to dissipate the suspicions which Dr Hort had expressed to me in private. We take it as proved that the scenery of Hermas' vision is actually laid in Arcadia, and we have not the slightest right to substitute Aricia, or to try to Italianize the vision.

Not only so, but as Mr Robinson has shewn by a number of considerations, the net result of the investigation is to shew that Hermas must have come from Arcadia; his geography is a part of himself and not a loan from Pausanias or some other guide-book. 'May he not,' asks Mr Robinson, 'have been a Greek slave of Arcadian origin? In this case his name, a common one for Greek slaves, would seem specially fitting for a native of this particular district, when we remember that Pausanias tells us of the worship of Hermas at Pheneos, twelve miles distant from Orchomenus..., when we remember also the story of the Nymphs who bathed him

at his birth in the sacred fountains of Trikrena, one of the spurs
of Mount Kyllene; and above all when we recall the epithet
'Cyllenius' derived from the worship of Hermas on the windless
summit of the great mountain-king of Arcadia, who reared his
head, as it was firmly believed, right up into the eternal calm
above the clouds and above the storms which darkened and
distressed the world at his feet.'

The conclusion seems to me to be correct as well as highly
eloquent; and I am quite prepared to admit that we have in
Hermas a Greek slave from Arcadia. And in this connexion, it is
worthy of note that it explains certain features in Hermas'
personal history. Arcadian slaves were commonly sold in pairs,
and we may get some light on the situation by recalling an
instance from the century before Hermas, where two brothers,
Arcadian slaves, rose to great eminence in the Roman Empire.
The case to which I allude is that of Pallas and Felix, who were
sold to Antonia, the mother of the emperor Claudius; both of
them attained their freedom; Pallas became a leading figure in
the life of imperial Rome, and Felix is known to us as the
procurator of Judaea who trembled before the preaching of Paul.
Now Tacitus tells us (*Ann.* xii. 53) that Pallas was 'regibus
Arcadiae ortus,' no doubt because he was named after one of the
Arcadian kings, Pallas the son of Lycaon; and if this be so, we
have an exact parallel to the naming of Hermas after the great
deity of Arcadia. But it may be asked, where is the brother of
Hermas to complete the parallel? The answer is in the Muratorian Canon which tells us that Hermas is the brother of Pius,
who occupied the episcopal chair of the Roman Church.

We thus arrive at a picturesque series of parallels between
the two pairs of Arcadian brothers, who, in two successive centuries,
attained eminence in Roman life; and while we do not wish to
press coincidences which may be accidental, such as the sale of
slaves to Roman ladies (cf. Herm. Vis. i. 1 ὁ θρέψας με πέπρακέν
με 'Ρόδῃ) and the like, we may at least illustrate by the successful
rise from slavery into political eminence of the two freedmen of
Claudius, the similar liberation which took place in the case of
Hermas and Pius, and which set one of them on the chair of
St Peter, and gave the other an even greater place than the chair
of Peter, as representative in the Church's literature of one of the
most interesting periods in her history.

ON THE ANGELOLOGY OF HERMAS.

(*Johns Hopkins University Circulars, April* 1884.)

THERE is a passage in the Shepherd of Hermas, Vis. iv. 2, 4, which has occasioned a great deal of perplexity to the commentators. Hermas is met by a fierce beast with a parti-coloured head, which beast symbolizes an impending persecution or tribulation, and makes as though it would devour him. But the Lord sends his angel who is over the wild beasts, whose name is Thegri, and shuts the mouth of the creature, that it may not hurt him.

Θεγρὶ according to Gebhardt and Harnack is 'nomen inauditum'; it appears in the Vulgate Latin as *Hegrin* and in the Palatine version as *Tegri*. The Ethiopic translation has *Tégêri*. Jerome seems to have read *Tyri*, since in his comments on Habac. i. 4 we have 'ex quo liber ille apocryphus stultitiae condemnandus est, in quo scriptum est quemdam angelum nomine Tyri praeesse reptilibus.' Much ingenuity has been expended over the origin of the word and in particular the following is the solution of Franciscus Delitzsch as given in Gebhardt and Harnack's edition : 'Si sumi possit, Hermam nomen angeli illius ex angelologia Judaica hausisse, quae angelos maris, pluviae, grandinis etc. finxit iisque nomina commentitia indidit, θεγρί idem est quod תִּגְרִי,

instimulator h. e. angelus, qui bestias (contra homines) instimulat atque, si velit, etiam domat (Taggar = dissidium, discordia ; cum î = Tigrî, quod bene descripsit H.: θεγρί etc.).'

I assent to the Hebrew origin of the name, but am unwilling to explain a *nomen inauditum* by a *nomen vix auditum*. A more simple solution presents itself; if for θ we write σ, according to the confusion common in uncial script, we have Σεγρὶ for the

name of the angel: which immediately suggests the root סָגַר,
to close. The angel is the one that *closes* or *shuts*. This is
immediately confirmed by the language of Hermas, ὁ κύριος
ἀπέστειλεν τὸν ἄγγελον αὐτοῦ τὸν ἐπὶ τῶν θηρίων ὄντα, οὗ τὸ
ὄνομά ἐστιν θεγρί, καὶ ἐνέφραξεν τὸ στόμα αὐτοῦ ἵνα μή σε
λυμάνῃ.

If any doubt remained as to the correctness of this solution it
would be swept away by reading the passage in Hermas side by
side with the LXX of Daniel vi. 23; ὁ θεός μου ἀπέστειλεν τὸν
ἄγγελον αὐτοῦ καὶ ἐνέφραξεν (וִסֲגַר) τὰ στόματα τῶν λεόντων
καὶ οὐκ ἐλυμήναντό με.

The curious parallelism of the language employed in the two
passages is decisive as to the etymology, and further we may be
sure that the language of Hermas is an indirect quotation from
the book of Daniel.

The result arrived at is an important one in many respects,
and has a possible bearing upon the genealogy of the MSS. and
versions of Hermas: so far as we are concerned we may simply
say that those copies and versions which read θεγρὶ or any
variation of the same bear conclusive marks of a Greek original.
It might seem unnecessary to make such a remark, but the fact is
that grave suspicions have been thrown out in some quarters as
to the character of the original text of Hermas. Upon further
consideration I am inclined indeed to conclude that all the versions
came from an original which read θεγρί, for even the Vulgate
Latin which has *Hegrin* seems to have arrived at it by dropping
the reduplicated T in the words

NOMEN EST THEGRI.

There is, however, another way in which the Latin variant
might be explained: for, as Dr Haupt points out to me, we have
a similar transformation in the Hebrew סְפַרְוָיִם (2 Kings xviii. 34)
which appears in Berosus as Σίσπαρα, in Ptolemy v. 18 Σίπφαρα,
but in Pliny vi. 123 as Hipparenum.

At this point the argument was taken up by Dr Hort, in a communication which appeared in the *Johns Hopkins University Circulars* for Dec. 1884, as follows:

Hermas and Theodotion;

a communication from Professor Hort with regard to an emendation of the text of Hermas.

The note on the Angelology of Hermas printed by Professor Rendel Harris in the *Johns Hopkins University Circular* for April contains a discovery of considerable interest in itself, and further noteworthy as having at once enabled the discoverer to find a satisfactory answer to an old riddle. There cannot be a doubt that he is right in tracing back the language of Hermas in Vis. iv. 2—4 to Daniel 6₂₂; and it is hardly less certain, I think, that he has given the true explanation of Θεγρὶ, the mysterious name of the angel who is sent to protect Hermas, by reading it as Σεγρὶ taken as a derivative from *sagar*, the verb employed in that verse for the shutting of the lions' mouths.

The best known repositories of Jewish angelology do not appear to contain the name of *Segri*: but Sigron (סגרון) is recorded by Lévy-Fleischer (p. 478) from the Talmudic Tract Sanhedrin as an accessory name of Gabriel, given him 'because, if he shuts the doors of heaven, no one can open them.' The designation would seem to belong more naturally in the first instance to some such high function as this than to the shutting of lions' mouths—an office not to be confounded with the general charge of lions or other beasts, said to have been appropriated to different angels; and the occurrence of Gabriel's name in Dan. 8₁₆; 9₂₁ may easily have been taken as determining the identity of the angel of 6₂₂. By what channel the Hebrew application of an obscure name belonging to Jewish tradition came to be accepted, though apparently misunderstood, by the Roman Hermas, is a question easier to ask than to answer.

My chief purpose, however, in writing this supplementary note, which is sent by Prof. Rendel Harris' request, is to point out that his discovery may have an important bearing on the disputed question of the Shepherd's date. The language of Hermas follows not the true Septuagint version of Daniel, but that of Theodotion, which superseded it in the course of the second century. The Septuagint drops the angel altogether: and in v. 22 has merely

$$\sigma\acute{\epsilon}\sigma\omega\kappa\acute{\epsilon}\nu \;\mu\epsilon \;\acute{o} \;\theta\epsilon\grave{o}\varsigma \;\acute{a}\pi\grave{o} \;\tau\hat{\omega}\nu \;\lambda\epsilon\acute{o}\nu\tau\omega\nu,$$

while it transfers the shutting of the lions' mouths to v. 18 by the insertion of an interpolated clause ending

$$\acute{a}\pi\acute{\epsilon}\kappa\lambda\epsilon\iota\sigma\epsilon\nu \;\tau\grave{a} \;\sigma\tau\acute{o}\mu\alpha\tau\alpha \;\tau\hat{\omega}\nu \;\lambda\epsilon\acute{o}\nu\tau\omega\nu \;\kappa\alpha\grave{\iota} \;o\grave{\upsilon} \;\pi\alpha\rho\eta\nu\acute{o}\chi\lambda\eta\sigma\alpha\nu \;\tau\hat{\omega} \;\Delta\alpha\nu\iota\acute{\eta}\lambda.$$

This clause, shortened in the opening words, was retained by Theodotion, with ἔκλεισεν (according to the best MSS.) substituted for ἀπέκλεισεν; but he corrected v. 22 by the Aramaic text reading ὁ θεός μου ἀπέστειλεν τὸν ἄγγελον αὐτοῦ καὶ ἐνέφραξεν τὰ στόματα τῶν λεόντων καὶ οὐκ ἐλυμήναντό με. Now Hermas has retained not only the angel, but the two characteristic Greek verbs, for he writes ὁ κύριος ἀπέστειλεν τὸν ἄγγελον αὐτοῦ...καὶ ἐνέφραξεν τὸ στόμα αὐτοῦ ἵνα μή σε λυμάνῃ.

It follows that Hermas cannot be older than Theodotion. To discuss the other evidence for the date of either Hermas or Theodotion would be beyond my present purpose.

F. J. A. HORT.

CAMBRIDGE, ENGLAND.
July 8, 1884.

This attempt to place the date of Hermas lower than that of Theodotion provoked the opposition of Dr Salmon who, in the following year in a note on Hermas and Theodotion which will be found appended to his Introduction to the New Testament, defended the antiquity of Hermas relatively to Theodotion. Dr Salmon had already in an article on Hermas in Smith's *Dictionary of Christian Biography* rejected the evidence of the Muratorian Canon which places the time of the composition of the Shepherd in the episcopate of Pius, i.e. c. A.D. 140—155. (The Canon itself must be later than this by some years, and we shall perhaps not be far wrong if we date it approximately in A.D. 180.) Salmon was now obliged to face new and, at first sight, conclusive evidence for the lateness of Hermas. True, the date of Theodotion is not a fixed point, being almost as much in dispute as the date of Hermas. But the evidence of the Patristic literature goes to shew that the Church abandoned the use of the Septuagint Daniel somewhere between the time of Justin and the time of Irenaeus, substituting for it the more exact version of Theodotion. And certainly the translation made by Theodotion is earlier than Irenaeus, for it is alluded to by the latter writer in his work against Heresies (iii. 21), and there are traces of the use of the Theodotion Daniel in the quotations of Irenaeus from the book itself. It follows, therefore, that Theodotion's text was known in the West as early as 180 A.D. And if we grant the use of Theodotion by Irenaeus why should we deny it in the case of Hermas?

The answer to this, from Dr Salmon's point of view, is that we have no right to assume that the only translations of Daniel current in the early Church were those of the LXX and of Theodotion. An examination of the quotations made from Daniel in the Apocalypse shews some singular agreements with the text of Theodotion as against the LXX, from which it is a natural inference that Theodotion remodelled an earlier version of Daniel. But in that case we have no right to say positively that Hermas has quoted from the text of Theodotion. Even in the very verse which is supposed to furnish the test case, we find a curious agreement with Daniel as quoted in the Epistle to the Hebrews, which suggests the use of a version like the Theodotion version by a writer a century earlier than Theodotion (cf. Heb. xi$_{33}$ ἔφραξαν στόματα λεόντων).

The argument must be traced at length in Dr Salmon's own pages, and it will, I think, leave the impression upon the mind of the student that a fair case has been made out for a suspense of judgment in regard to inferences drawn from the Segri passage. Probably it will also be felt that Dr Salmon went too far when he suggested that even the quotations in Irenaeus, which were supposed to come from Theodotion, might be from some lost early version to which that of Theodotion was closely related. If these quotations are to be disputed, in the light of the known fact of Irenaeus' acquaintance with the version of Theodotion, we should almost be obliged to go further, and deny the use of Theodotion by Irenaeus' pupil Hippolytus. But this step is too extreme for any one who was not prepared to abolish Theodotion altogether. But without denying the use of Theodotion by Irenaeus we might hold the posteriority of Hermas to be *non-proven*, and the question then arises as to whether there is any further light to be obtained upon the disputed points from fresh points of view.

PRESTER JOHN'S LIBRARY.

*A Lecture delivered in the Divinity School, Cambridge,
in October* 1892.

THE newspapers have from time to time during the last two
years informed us that the King of Abyssinia has begun to collect
books for a Royal Library, and that he has made requisition from
the monks of the various monasteries in his kingdom for the
leading works which are extant among them, or for copies of
the same. One suspects that some traveller is there who has
been urging the King to make collections with the view of
rendering the recovery of lost Ethiopic books more easy. If that
be so, he is a wise traveller and deserves our best thanks.

The suggestion, however, of a royal library for Abyssinia takes
us back as well as invites us forward; for one of the features
of the great kingdom of Prester John, the Christian King of
Ethiopia, whom the Portuguese discovered holding the faith in
the mountains that border on the southern end of the Red Sea,
was a magnificent library. Abyssinia was reported to be a
paradise of books, as well as a Christian country with a Happy
Valley in it[1]. And the description which the English writer
Purchas gives of this collection of rare books is enough to make
the mouth of every scholar and bibliophile to water. Let me
draw your attention, as mine has been drawn by a friend, to the
following extract from *Purchas his Pilgrimage or Relations of the*

---

[1] Rasselas is no mere imagination of Johnson; he wrote the novel shortly after
he had been doing the hack-work of translating Lobo's *Voyage to Abyssinia* for
Bettesworth and Hicks of Paternoster Row, who published it in 1735. Johnson
received five guineas for this piece of work and devoted his first earnings to the
funeral expenses of his mother. The translation was made from the French
edition.

World and the Religions observed in all Ages, London, 1613;
pp. 565 ff., Of the Hill Amara: and the rarities therein. After
describing the natural features of the hill, the stately buildings
of the two churches with their monasteries, he goes on to speak of
the library thus (p. 567):

"In the monastery of the Holy Crosse are two rare peeces,
whereon Wonder may justly fasten both her eies; the Treasury
and Library[1] of the Emperour, neither of which is thought to be
matchable in the world. That Librarie of Constantinople[2] wherein
were 120000 bookes, nor the Alexandrian Library, wherein
Gellius[3] numbereth 700000, had the fire not been admitted (too
hastie a student) to consume them, yet had they come short, if
report over-reach not, this whereof we speake, their number is in
a maner innumerable, their price inestimable. The Queene of
Saba (they say) procured Bookes hither from all parts, besides
many which Solomon gave her, and from that time to this, their
Emperors have succeeded in like care and diligence. There are
three great Halls, each above two hundred paces large, with Bookes
of all Sciences, written in fine parchment, with much curiosity
of golden letters, and other workes, and cost in the writing,
binding, and covers: some on the floore, some on shelves about
the sides; there are few of paper: which is but a new thing in
Ethiopia[4]. There are the writings of Enoch copied out of the
stones wherein they were engraven, which intreate of Philosophie,
of the Heavens and Elements. Others goe under the name of
Noe, the subject whereof is Cosmographie, Mathematickes, cere-
monies and prayers; some of Abraham which he composed when
he dwelt in the valley of Mamre, and there read publikely Philosophie and the Mathematikes. There is very much of Salomon,
a great number passing under his name; many ascribed to Job,
which he writ after the recovery of his property[5]; many of Esdras,
the Prophets and high Priests. And besides the four canonicall
Gospels, many others ascribed to Bartholmew, Thomas, Andrew,
and many others; much of the Sibylles, in verse and prose; the

---

[1] "The library of the Prete." [Margin.]   [2] "Zonar. Ann. to. 3." [Margin.]
[3] "Gell. li. 6 c. 17." [Margin.]
[4] "Fr. Luys hath a very large catalogue of them l. 1, c. 9 taken out (as he saith)
of an Index, wh. Anthony Gricus and L. Cremones made of them, being sent
hither by the Pope Gregory 13 at the instance of Cardinall Zarlet, which sawe and
admired the varietie of them, as did many others then in their company." [Margin.]
[5] Qu. prosperity.

workes of the Queen of Saba; the Greek Fathers all that have
written, of which many are not extant with us; the writers of
Syria, Egypt, Africa, and the Latine Fathers translated, with
others innumerable in the Greeke, Hebrew, Arabike, Abissine,
Egyptian, Syrian, Chaldee, far more authors, and more of them
than we have; few in Latin; yet T. Livius is there whole, which
with us is imperfect, and some of the works of Thomas Aquinas;
Saint Augustines workes are in Arabike: Poets, Philosophers, Physicians, Rabbines, Talmudists, Cabalistes, Hierogliphikes, and others
would be too tedious to relate. When Jerusalem was destroyed
by Titus; when the Saracens over-ranne the Christian world;
many books were conveyed out of the Eastern partes into Ethiopia;
when Ferdinand and Isabella expelled the Jewes out of Spaine,
many of them entered Ethiopia and for doing this without licence,
enriched the Pretes library with their Bookes; when Charles V
restored Muleasses to his kingdom, the Prete hearing that there
was at Tunis a great Library sent and bought more than 3000
books of divers arts. There are about 200 monks whose office
it is to looke to the Librarie, to keep them cleane and sound; each
appointed to the Books of that language which he understandeth;
the Abbot hath streight charge from the Emperor, to have care
thereof, he esteeming this Library more than his treasure."

The foregoing statements of Purchas are astonishing enough,
and it may well be supposed that the range of the literature
declared to be extant in the library of Prester John would be
sufficient, of itself, to destroy all faith in the authority of the
narrator: and indeed this seems to have been the impression
produced upon the minds of many scholars of the day, who, while
they were not unwilling to believe that lost books might be
recovered from Abyssinian libraries, not unnaturally shrank from
the belief that all the lost works of ancient Christian literature,
to say nothing of pagan letters, were to be found under a single
roof in the library of Rasselas.

But we must admit that the statements made by Purchas
have an air of verisimilitude to a modern scholar. Take the
very first statement made by the Elizabethan writer, that the
books are all on vellum, and that paper is a new thing in Ethiopia.
Does that look like an invention? Take Wright's Catalogue of
the Ethiopic MSS. in the British Museum: and examine whether
there are any paper MSS. You will find that they are sur-

prisingly few, and of those which exist almost all are of a more recent date than Purchas' Pilgrims: e.g. No. 127 is written in the xviiith century; No. 151 is dated 1630; No. 318 was written in the xixth century; No. 357 was written about the beginning of the xixth century; No. 392 was written in A.D. 1861; No. 395 was written in 1810 (and the paper is dated 1807), and so on. In fact I have not noted any copy in the British Museum on paper which was not written later than Purchas' day. Is not this remarkable? How did Purchas' informant know that things were so different in Abyssinia to what they were in Syria, for example?

In the next place notice that the first of the books referred to by Purchas as extant in the Abyssinian Library is " the writings of Enoch, copied out of the stones on which they were engraven, which intreate of Philosophie, of the Heavens and Elements." Is it not strange that the front rank should have been assigned to the very book which was actually brought back a century and a half later from Abyssinia by the traveller Bruce? Further the reference to the heavenly tablets is in agreement with the language of the book of Enoch; for example, compare c. 81 "and he said unto me, O Enoch, observe the writing of the heavenly tablets, and read what is written thereon and mark every individual fact. And I observed everything on the heavenly tablets, and read everything which was written thereon and understood everything." Compare with it the manner in which the book of Enoch is cited in the Testament of the Twelve Patriarchs: "and now, O my sons, I have read in the tablets of heaven."

Last of all the description which Purchas gives is not a bad summary of the contents of the lost book. The most recent editor of Enoch (Mr Charles) describes a certain section of the book as a Book of Celestial Physics, which is not unlike Purchas' language concerning the Heavens and the Elements. For example, the 62nd chapter entitles itself "The Book of the courses of the luminaries of the heaven and the relations of each, according to their classes &c."

It must, I think, be admitted that Purchas' account of the book of Enoch is not inconsistent with the belief that he derived his knowledge from some one who had seen the book.

A little lower down in the list we are told that the library contained the works of the Queen of Saba. Now this, at all

events, could hardly have been derived from notices of the earlier
Greek and Latin literature. The Queen of Sheba, however, is one
of the stock figures in Abyssinian History; for instance in the
book called Kebra Nagast (the Glory of Kings) fourteen chapters
are devoted to the legends concerning the Queen of Sheba[1].
Further the Abyssinian literature contains amongst the laws and
statutes of the kingdom, a collection brought from Jerusalem
by Menelek the son of Solomon. Menelek's mother is the Queen
of Sheba.

Now we can hardly regard it as a pure accident that Purchas
has thrust the Queen of Sheba in amongst the ecclesiastical
authors known in Abyssinia; he must have had some knowledge
or tradition at the very least with regard to the historical and
literary position assigned to the elect lady in question by the
Abyssinians.

It becomes proper for us, therefore, to investigate as far as
possible the sources from which Purchas drew his wonderful
account of the Ethiopian literature.

Now, as will be seen from our quotation, Purchas gives a
marginal reference which betrays his authority: he tells us that
" Fr. Luys hath a very large catalogue of them (the Abyssinian
treasures) taken out, as he saith, of an Index, which Anthony
Gricus and L. Cremoncs made of them, being sent hither by the
Pope Gregory 13 at the instance of Cardinall Zarlet, which sawe
and admired the varietie of them, as did many others then in
their company."

Cardinal Zarlet is, of course, the famous Sirletus, Librarian of
the Vatican, and just the very man to have instituted a literary
hunt in connexion with the Apostolic missions to the Ethiopes.
But who is Fr. Luys, that tells the tale?

Amongst the historians who have written of Ethiopia in
modern times, we find the name of Luys de Urreta. His work
'Historia de la Etiopia' was published at Valencia in the year
1610, just three years before the first edition of Purchas. In
those days Englishmen travelled in Spain and talked Spanish
and read Spanish. One has only to recall the allusions in
Shakespeare to Spanish customs and the borrowing of Spanish
words in a manner which would be unintelligible now-a-days

---

[1] These chapters were edited by Pretorius in 1870 under the title 'Fabula de
Regina Sabaca apud Æthiopes.'

and to compare similar phenomena in Ben Jonson and other
Elizabethan writers, in order to assure oneself that in the golden
age of English literature learned men were familiar with Spanish[1].
There is then no difficulty *a priori* in the use of a Spanish
author by Purchas, two or three years after the date of production
of his work. But we need not speculate, for we have only to read
Purchas side by side with Fr. Luys de Urreta in order to see that
practically everything in the one is translated from the other.
The very description of the Monasteries, and their location on the
sacred mountain of Amara, comes out of Urreta, and so does the
whole account of the library and its contents.

In proof of these statements we transcribe some sentences of
Urreta, and reproduce his account of the Library, from which
it will be seen that it is indeed, as Purchas described it, a *very
large catalogue*, too large apparently for the faith of Purchas,
and his was no slight faith, to judge from the number of lost
books which he advertised out of Urreta.

In lib. i. c. 9 Urreta tells us all about Prester John's library
under the heading De los dos Monasterios que ay nel Monte
Amarà, y la famosa libreria que tiene en uno de ellos el Preste
Juan....Estas dos Iglesias que la una se intitula del Espiritu
Santo, y la otra de Santa Cruz, son las mas sumptuosas y
magnificas q̄ ay en toda la Etiopia.

He then gives a sketch of the most famous libraries in the
world, from Aulus Gellius, Epiphanius, Plutarch, Galen, Nicephorus
and Zonaras. Two of his references, viz. to Zonaras and Gellius
will be found on the margin of Purchas. He goes on to describe
the buildings: *Son tres salas grandissimas, cada una de mas
de dozientos passos de largo*, donde ay libros de todas scientias,
todos en pergamino muy sutiles, delgados y bruñidos, con mucha
curiosidad de lettras doradas y otras labores y lindezas; unos
enquadernados ricamente, con sus tablas; otros estan sueltos,
como processos, rollados y metidos dentro de unas bolsas y talegas
de tafetan: *de papel ay muy pocos, y es cosa moderna y muy nueva
entra los de Etiopia.*

The passages which I have printed in italics shew the source
from which Purchas derived his information about the size of the

---

[1] Cf. George Herbert's playful allusion:

"It cannot sing or play the lute,
It never was in France *or Spain*."

three separate halls, and the predominance of vellum books over
paper, and the whole of his statements may be further compared
with Urreta.

Next comes the Catalogue made for Gregory XIII.

El aranzel que se traxo al Sumo Pontifice Gregorio decimotercio, es el siguiente. Hay escrituras de *Enoch*, q̄ fue el
septimo nieto de Adam, las quales estā en pergaminos, façadas
de piedras y ladrillos donde se escriuieron primeramente, que tratan
de cosas de Philosophia, de cielos y elementos. Hay otros libros
q̄ van cõ nombre de *Noe*, que tratā de Cosmographia, y Matematicas d̄ cosas naturales y de algunas oraciones y ceremonias.
Hay libros de *Abraham*, los que el compuso quando estuuo en el
valle de Mambre, donde tenia discipulos y leya publicamente
Philosophia y las Mathematicas; estos discipulos fueron con cuya
ayuda vencio a los quatro Reyes que lleuauan preso a su sobrino
Loth. De *Salomon* muchissimos, unos traydos por la Reyna Saba,
otros por Melilec hijo de Salomon, y otros q̄ el mismo Rey Salomon
embiaua, y assi son en grande numero los que van con titulo de
Salomon. Hay muchos libros con titulo de *Job*, y dizen que el los
compuso despues que boluio en su antigua prosperidad.

So far we can see that Purchas has taken practically everything in Urreta. But it will be noticed that Urreta is not
destitute of information which could not have been obtained
except from people conversant with Ethiopian life. The allusion
to Melilec the son of Solomon agrees closely with what we have
noted above from the Kebra Nagast or book of the Glory of Kings.

Urreta continues as follows; and we shall see that Purchas is
with him for a part of the account:

Hay muchos libros de *Esdras*, y de muchos *Prophetas y Sumos
Sacerdotes*. Muchas epistolas extraordinarias de *San Pablo*[1], de las
quales no se tiene en la Europa noticia. Muchos Evangelios fuera
de los quatro Canonicos y Sagrados, que son san Matheo, san Lucas,
san Marcos, y san Juan, como *el Evangelio secundum Hebraeos,
secundum Nazaraeos, Encratitas, Ebionitas, y Egipcios;* y Evangelio
secundum Bartholomaeum, Andream, S. Thomam, y otros.

Compare this with Purchas' account, and you will see that the
English transcriber has begun to abbreviate. Urreta's account
grows more and more wonderful.

---

[1] The italicized authors are either those mentioned above by Purchas, or they are
names to which we shall refer a little later on. See note on p. 40.

Aunque es verdad que todos estos Evangelios y libros nombrados sean apocriphos, de muy poca, o ninguna autoridad, con todo los pongo aqui por curiosidad que por tal los guardan en esta libreria, que tambien los tienen por apocriphos en toda la Etiopia; solo los guardan por grandeza, y lo es sin duda para una libreria. Hay muchos libros de *las Sybillas* en verso y en prosa, y otros compuestos por *la reyna Saba y Melilec.*

By this time Purchas had got as much as he could carry, and he summarizes what remains in Urreta, by telling us that all the Greek and Latin fathers, and all the Philosophers, Physicians and Rabbis are there. Urreta's account proceeds as follows:

Historias de la vida y muerte de Jesu Christo, y otras cosas que sucedieron despues de su muerte, compuestas por algunos Judios de aquellos tiempos. Hay tambien muchos libros de Abdias[1], San Dionysio, fuera de los que por Europa tienen de Origines, y de su maestro Clemente Alexandrino, y el maestro de este Panteno, de todos estos ay muchas obras; de solo Origines ay mas de dozientos libros. Tertulliano, san Basilio, san Cypriano, san Cyrillo, san Hilario, san Hilarion, san Anastasio, san Gregorio Niceno, y Nazianzeno, Epiphanio Damaceno, y todos los Dotores Griegos, sin que aya ninguno de los que han escrito que no este en esta libreria: no solo los que comunmente andan entra las manos, pero otros muy esquisitos que no se tiene de ellos noticia, cōpuestos per los mismos Dotores. De San Ephrem Siro, Moyses Bar cepha, y de otros de la Iglesia Syra. Muchos tomos de San Juan Chrisostomo, y de su maestro Diodoro Tarcēse todas sus obras. Oecumenio, Doroteo, Tyro[2], y Dionysio Alexandrino discipulo de Origines. Serapion en muchos libros, San Justino Martyr muchas obras, con las de su discipulo Taciano; todos los Theodoros, el Antiocheno, el Heracleyta, y el Syro, o Teodorito por otro nombre, en compañia de Theodolo; los dos Zacharias, el Obispo de Hierocesarea, y el de Chrisopolis, *Triphon discipulo de Origines; y Tito Bostrense Arabio.* Tambien estan las obras de *Ticonio* y Arnobio, Theophilato Antiocheno: las obras de Theognosto alabado por San Athanasio, y Theodoto Ancirano, Acacio discipulo de Eusebio Cesariense, San Alberto Carmelita, Alexandro de Capadocia; las obras de Ammonio Alexandrino maestro de Origines, y las de Amphilochio de Iconio, que tuuo la ciencia

---

[1] Cp. lib. ii. c. 14 "Abdias in vita Apostolorum."
[2] I follow the punctuation of the MS.

reuelada; Anastasio Sinayta, y el Anastasio Antiocheno, y Andreas
el Cretense, y Hierosolimitano, y el Cesariense, Antiocho Monacho,
y Antiocho Ptolemaydo, Antipater Bostrense; los dos Apollinares,
el Junior y el Antiquior; y tambien los dos Aristobolos, el moço y
el viejo, y Aretas Cesariense, *Rodon discipulo de Taciano, Rodul-
pho Agricola, Cayo Mario, Victorino, Catina, Syro, por su nombre
Lepos, esto es, agudo, ingenioso;* Proclo Constantinopolitano,
*Primacio Uticense discipulo de San Augustin, Policronio discipulo
de Diodoro, Phocion, y Pierio Alexandrino, Philon Judio,* del
qual ay mas de trezientos libros, cosa que admiro. Y los Judios de
Egipto, de Arabia, y otras partes se obligā a dar muchos millares
de ducados, solo por que se las dexen trasladar. *Pedro Edesino
discipulo de San Efren, Paulo Emesino, y Patrophilo Palestino,
Pantaleon;* de san *Didimo Alexandrino* ay muchos libros, y
tambien son muchos los *de Egesippo: Oresieso Etiope Monge, que
vivio año* 420; y las obras de *Olimpiodoro* y de san Nilo y
muchas de Nepote Egipcio: Euagrio Antiocheno, y las obras de
Eudoxia Emperatriz muger de Theodosio el menor; Euthalion
Monge, Basilio, Eustachio Antiocheno, y Euthimio y san Metho-
dio, las obras de Melito Sardense, y de San Luciano Antiocheno, y
de *Flauiano Constantinopolitano,* y *Fortunaciano Africano,* y el
glorioso *Fulgencio, Junilio,* y *Julio, todos Africanos;* los libros de
*Judas Syro, Isidoro Pelusiota en Egipto, discipulo de San Chriso-
stomo, Isidoro Thesalonicense;* estan las obras *de George Trape-
zuncio,* y de *Gennadio Constantinopolitano;* los dos *Josephos,*
San Juan Climaco, y Cassiano, *Hisichio Hierosolimitano;* de San
Augustin ay inumerables obras, no solo las que comunmente
andan por las librerias, sin otros muchos libros que nunca se han
impresso: de San Hieronymo, San Ambrosio, San Leon Papa, y
San Gregorio Magno ay algunos libros, aunque muy pocos, porque
de los Dotores Latinos es lo menos que ay. Y aduiertase, que
todos los libros que ay en estas tres salas son en lingua Griega,
Arabiga, Egipcia, Sira, Chaldea, Hebrea, y Abissina: en lingua
Latina no auia ningun libro, sino todas las Decadas de Titoliuio,
que por la Europa no se tenian, y alla estauan oluidadas, que como
no las sabian leer, no hazian caso de ellas. Lo que digo de los
libros de Dotores Latinos, estauan traduzidos en lengua Griega,
como San Hieronymo, Ambrosio, San Augustin en lingua Arabiga.
De los Dotores mas modernos ay algunos, como las partes de
Santo Thomas, y el *Contra Gentes:* las Obras de San Antonino, y

el directorio Inquisitorum, traduzidas en lingua Abissina por
Pedro Abbas Abissin, natural de Etiopia, hombre doctissimo en
lenguas y Theologia Escolastica, traduxo muchas sumas de casos de
conciencia, y cada dia se van traduziendo obras de Latin, Italiano,
Español en el collegio de los Indianos en Roma, para embiar a la
Etiopia; y al presente se estan traduziendo en lengua Etiopia las
obras deuotas de Fray Luys de Granada. Estan sobra la Sagrada
Escritura todas las translaciones de Origenes, Luciano, Theodosion,
Simacho, Aquila; liciones Griegas, Arabigas, Egipcias, Hebreas,
Chaldeas, Abissinas, en Armenio, y en Persa, tambien esta la
Latina; pero la Vulgata que se cita, y lee, es la Chaldea[1]. De
Astrologia, Matematicas, Medicina, Philosophia, son innumerabiles
los libros que ay escritos en las linguas dichas, Platon, Aristoteles,
Pitagoras, Zenon; de Archimedes, Auicena, Galeno, Hipocrates,
Auerroes, muchos libros, no solo los que comunmente se platican,
sino otros muchos, de los quales no se tiene por aca noticia.
Libros de Poetas como Homero, Pindaro, innumerabiles. De
historias ay gran numero. Basta dezir que los libros que ay son
mas de un million. De Rabinos assi antes de la venida de
Christo, como despues de su santissima muerte, ay muchissimos;
como de Rabi Dauid Kimki, Rabi Moyses Aegyptius, Moyses
Hadarsam, Sahadias, Bengion, Rabi Salomon, Simeon Benjochay,
Simeon Benjoachim, Rabi Abraham, Benesra, Bacaiay, Chischia,
Abraham Parizol, Abraham Saua, Rab. Achaigool, Rabi Ammay,
Rab. Baruchias, Rab. Isaac, Ben Scola, Isaac Karo, Isaac Nathan,
Rab. Ismael, Rab. Leui Bengerson, Rab. Pacieta, y otros muchos.
De la Cabala, y del Talmud de los Judios auia en un aposento mas
de cinco mil tomos. Esta tabla que he puesto en este capitulo es
parte de un indice y aranzel que hizo de todos ellos Antonio
Greco, y Lorenço Cremones, embiados por el Papa Gregorio
decimotercio, a instancia del Cardinal Zarleto: los quales fueron a
la Etiopia solo para reconocer la libreria, en compañia de otros
que eran embiados para lo proprio, y vinieron admirados de ver
tantos libros, que en su vida vieron tantos juntos, y todos de mano
y en pergamino, y todos muy grandes, porque son como libros de
coro, con el pergamino entero, con los estantes de Cedro muy
curioso, y en tan diferentes linguas.

---

[1] That is the Ethiopic: cf. letter of Gonzalez Roderico to the Jesuits in Goa,
quoted in Purchas lib. vii. c. 8 "I had made my book in Portuguese and it was
necessary to turn it into Chaldee." It is also so named in the *Psalterium in qua-
tuor linguis* of 1518.

Urreta goes on, after this tremendous catalogue, to tell us how all these books got to Abyssinia, beginning with the Queen of Sheba, and working down through various historical persecutions and falls of great cities with subsequent removals of collections of books and the like.

Now what are we to say to all this story?

Is there anything in it and how much? We have noticed already that the suspicions awakened in favour of the genuineness of Purchas' story are not reduced to nothing by reading the accounts of Urreta. There are some things brought to light which betray an actual knowledge of Abyssinia. He tells us, moreover, what, as a member of the Dominican order he ought to know, and which is probably quite correct, that the Roman missionaries were translating various books of doctrine and discipline into Ethiopic, such as the works of Aquinas or S. Luys de Granada. And he says that his lists are taken from catalogues made at the instigation of Sirletus. All of this looks reasonable enough, if it were not for the colossal size of the library and its wonderful inclusiveness. What are we to say to it?

We know what was said by contemporary writers.

Urreta's account was challenged by Godignus in his book *De Abassinorum rebus*, published at Lyons in 1615.

Godignus says (lib. i. cap. xvii.) "Ait in monte Amara, in coenobio sanctae crucis eam (bibliotecam) servari, et ab Regina Sabae accepisse initium, repositos ibi esse libros permultos, quos et tunc Salomon ipsi reginae ab Hierosolymis in patriam discedenti dono dedit: et singulis deinde annis solitus erat ad eandem mittere. Inter reliquos esse quosdam, quos vetustissimus ille Enochus ab Adamo septimus de coelo de elementis etc....

Haec de monstruosa illa biblioteca dixisse satis. Reliqua apud eum videat, qui volet. Duo tamen hic adjungenda quae addit. Unum est, Sirleti Cardinalis rogatu, fuisse a Gregorio xiii Pontifice maximo in Ethiopiam missos Antonium Gricum et Laurentium Cremonensem, ut hanc inspicerent bibliotecam etc....

Haec ille. Sed nullam in monte Amara esse bibliotecam, ex litteris habemus, et narratione eorum, qui loca illa diu coluere. Nonnihil librorum est in eo coenobio, quod Axumum vel Acaxumum dicitur, et a regina Candace ferunt aedificatum in urbe Saba, quae nunc paene euersa, et aequata solo nonnulla retinet antiquae signa pulchritudinis. Quidquid id tamen librorum est, regiae bibliotecae non meretur nomen.

Ita referunt, qui rem perpexere, indubitatae homines fidei." It may perhaps be thought that Godignus was a little too sweeping in his condemnations; no doubt the Jesuit fathers were not disposed to regard with much confidence the statements of the Friars Preachers with regard to Abyssinia or any other matter. Godignus' contemptuous rejection of Urreta was taken up by Ludolf in his History of Ethiopia, published not long after. I quote the second English edition, which bears the date 1684. Ludolf says:

"Besides sacred books the Habessines have but very few others. For the story of Barratti[1], who chatters of a library containing ten thousand volumes, 'tis altogether vain and frivolous. Some few we had an account of," and he appends the following note:

"Urreta did not think worth while to tell so modest an untruth. The most celebrated Libraries, saith he, that ever had renown were nothing in respect of Presbyter John's: the books are without number, richly and artificially bound; many to which Solomon's and the Patriarchs' names are affixt. Godignus explodes him, l. i. c. 17."

Quétif, the literary historian of the Dominicans, in giving an account of the works of Fr. Luys de Urreta, endeavours to apologize for a description of Abyssinia which he has not courage to defend by suggesting that Urreta was imposed upon by some Ethiopian. He had no intention himself to utter anything that was not truth, but some one played off on him a literary forgery.

"De quibus operibus (sc. Urretae) eruditi alii aliter sentiunt, nos hoc unum contendimus Urretam ab implanatorum falsariorumve crimine immunem esse, nec quid quod verum ipse non putaret edidisse: utrum autem cujusdam Aethiopis agyrtae Joannis Baltazar[2] fraudibus illectus et circumventus fuerit, faciliorisque fidei hominem se praestiterit, ac levioris, id peritorum certe cordatorumque relinquimus arbitrio et criterio."

---

[1] John Nunez Barreti (a Portuguese of the city of Oporto) was appointed Patriarch of Ethiopia by the influence of King John of Portugal and at the instance of Peter the Abyssinian: his life will be found in the second book of Godignus, *De Abassinorum rebus:* cf. Purchas, *Pilgrims,* lib. vii. c. 8.

[2] This John Balthazar Abassinus is alluded to in Godignus lib. ii. c. 18, p, 315. Purchas lib. vii. c. 8 (ed. 1625) speaks of him and his connexion with Urreta in the following decided manner: "One Juan de Baltasar, a pretended Abassine, and Knight of the Militarie Order of Saint Antonie, hath written a Booke in Spanish of that Order, founded (as he saith) by the Prete John, in the daies of Saint Basil, with

But this appeal for mercy leaves us still without an explanation of the way in which the fraud, if it was indeed a fraud, was concocted by the hypothetical Ethiopian. It certainly was no ordinary person that manufactured the catalogue in the first instance. To take a single specimen, we are told that the library contained an account of the events occurring in connexion with the Passion, and subsequently; this evidently means the Gospel of Nicodemus, but the writer goes on to say that it was an account written by the Jews: this arises out of the false prologue to the Nicodemus Gospel which affirms the Hebrew origin of the legends. But the reference implies a writer who had also read carefully the books which be describes. Would an Ethiopic trickster have done it so cleverly as this? Why may not the Acts of Pilate have been extant in Abyssinia?

We will now try to take the enquiry a little further, by pointing out the actual source from which Urreta's lists are derived.

It has occurred to me that perhaps the details may be extracted from the Biblioteca of Sixtus Senensis: and I now propose to shew that this is really the case. The supposition is not an unlikely one, for Sixtus is the great scholar of the Dominican order; moreover, there is on the margin of Urreta's book, in one place, a reference to Sixtus. He is describing the works of the Patriarchs who wrote before the Flood, and on the margin are the words

Escrituras hechas antea del diluvio

Sixto Senense lib 4. Bibliothecae.

Our main reason for making this suggestion lies in the fact that Urreta's list has every appearance of being taken from an alphabetically arranged catalogue. For example, we have such conjunctions as:

Tatian: Theodorus Ant.: Theodorus Heracl.: Theodorus Syrus: Theodoritus: Theodoulos:

rules received from him, above seven hundred yeares before any Military Order was in the world. I know not whether his Booke (which I have by me) hath more lies or lines; a man of a leaden braine and a brazen face; seconded, if not exceeded by the Morall, Naturall and Politicall Historie of Ethiopia, the worke of his Scholler Luys d'Urreta, a Spanish Frier and lyer: the said Godignus every where through his first Booke confutes him."

I have examined Baltazar's book, published at Valencia in 1609, entitled *Fundacion, Vida y Regla de la grande orden militar*, and do not see any reason to make him responsible for Urreta in the matter of the Catalogue.

and then after inserting Zacharias of Hierocesarea and Zacharias of Chrysopolis, we go on with Tryphon, Titus of Bostra, and Ticonius and so on.

The list then inserts Arnobius, and returns to the end of the alphabet with Theophylact, and Theognostus.

There is a method in this madness; it is not necessary to spend time in making illustrations of it. Where is the catalogue from which this was taken? Either the books in the library of Prester John were arranged alphabetically, and followed a Western alphabet, or we have here a Western book catalogue from which selections have been made. That the latter is the solution appears at once on consulting Sixtus Senensis.

Let us take one or two extracts from Urreta, and put side by side with them the corresponding parts of the alphabetically arranged catalogue of Sixtus.

Urreta	*Sixtus*
Triphon discipulo de Origenes y Tito Bostrense Arabio. Tambien estan las obras de Ticonio.	Titus Bostrenae ecclesiae in Arabia episcopus. Triphon, Origenis discipulus. Tichonius, natione Afer.
Acacio, discipulo de Eusebio Cesariense, San Alberto Carmelita, Alexandro de Capadocia.	Acacius...Caesariensis Ecclesiae Palestinae episcopus, Eusebii Caesariensis Episcopi discipulus. Albertus Joannis Harlemensis Carmelita.... Alexander, Episcopus Cappadociae.

(The intrusion of the modern writer between the two Church Fathers is very striking.)

Rodon discipulo de Taciano, Rodulpho Agricola,	Rhodon Asianus, Tatiani in scripturis auditor et discipulus, followed by Rodolphus Agricola, Frisius.
Cayo Mario, Victorino,	Caius Marius Victorinus Afer, rhetor sui temporis praestantissimus. And a little later on,
Catina Syro, por su nombre Lepos, esto es, agudo, ingenioso.	Catina Syrus, cognomine Leptos, id est, acutus et ingeniosus...Cuius meminit Hieronymus libro i. comm. in Ezech., referens summatim expositionem illius super visione rotarum et animalium.

Or compare the following:

Oresieso Etiope Monge, que vivio año 420 y las obras de Olimpiodoro.	Oresiesis monachus et eremita, Pachomii et Theodori monachorum in solitudinibus Ægypti commorantium collega...Claruit sub Honorio Aug. anno Dom. 420.... Olympiodorus Monachus.

But we need not occupy more space in proving what is abundantly clear that the list of Urreta is a series of extracts from Sixtus Senensis, and that he follows his authority even in printers' errors[1]. We can hardly interpose another writer between Urreta and Sixtus, and the idea that the catalogue was the fabrication of an Ethiopian monk seems especially improbable.

The only question that remains is whether Urreta has drawn upon the narratives of the Dominican missionaries as well as upon the printed work to which we have tracked him. This is not at all an unlikely supposition, and deserves looking into. But we must first subtract all the information that can fairly be set down to Sixtus: and when this is done, there is very little left. All the lost Gospels are gone, Livy is gone, Abraham, and Noah and

---

[1] The following further coincidences may be noted with passages which we have italicized in Urreta's account.

Tryphon, Origenis discipulus,

preceded by

Titus Bostrenae ecclesiae in Arabia episcopus.

and a little earlier

Tichonius, natione Afer.

Primasius, Uticensis in Africa episcopus, divi Augustini, ut creditur discipulus, Pierius, Alexandrinae ecclesiae presbyter... Placidus... Polychronius...Diodori Tarsensis episcopi auditor...

and on an earlier page

Petrus, Edessenae Ecclesiae presbyter, scripsit in morem Sancti Ephrem Syro sermone Homilias etc....

and on the previous page

Paulus, Emesae episcopus,

and a little earlier

Patrophilus Scythopoleos, Palaestinae episcopus,

and on the previous page

Pantaleon, magnae Dei ecclesiae diaconus etc.

The reader can also verify a host of other names, both those which we have italicized and most of the others. From Sixtus comes also the table of Rabbis.

Enoch have disappeared, and the crowd of lesser men. Prester John's Library has shrunk to quite an attenuated form, and we are now in danger of expecting nothing from Abyssinia instead of expecting everything. A winter of discontent has followed rapidly on the glorious summer of Urreta's promises. We are reduced from the stately palace of Rasselas to a lodge in a garden of cucumbers. The attitude of despair is, however, as unreasonable as that of extreme hope. The libraries which gave us Enoch and the Book of Jubilees cannot be exhausted. It is not generally known that the English army swept up nearly 1000 MSS. at the capture of Magdala, and left 600 of them behind in a church on their return to the sea-coast[1].

It is much to be regretted that no sufficient band of Ethiopic scholars was attached to the Abyssinian expedition. Were those 600 volumes all prayer-books?

These books from the collection of king Theodore cannot, however, be held to have exhausted the MS. wealth of Abyssinia. And significant rumours have lately been reaching us of discoveries made in an island on one of the great Abyssinian lakes.

Here is a notice from a German paper of March 16, 1894 (*Theol. Lit.-Blatt*): "König Menelek von Abessinien hat, nach der Meldung französischer Blätter, bei einer Expedition nach dem im Süden seines Reiches gelegenen Zuai-See einen werthvollen Fund alt-äthiopischer Manuskripte gemacht. Die Inseln dieses Sees galten immer als 'heilig' und die dortige schwer nahbare Bevölkerung verwahrt trotz ihrer barbarischen Unbildung nach alter Ueberlieferung die äthiopischen Bücher als Heiligthümer. Die auf der Insel Debra-Sina gemachten Funde sind theils liturgischen Inhalts, zum anderen Theil versprechen sie aber werthvollere Ausbeute. Der König beabsichtigt eine Dampferverbindung auf dem See herzustellen, womit der sagenhafte Zauber der heiligen Inseln verschwinden würde."

[1] *Record of the Expedition to Abyssinia*, ii. 396: "On the capture of Magdala a large number of Ethiopian MSS. were found, having been carried there by Theodore from the libraries of Gondar and the central parts of Abyssinia during his late expedition, in which he destroyed very many Christian churches. On finding that Magdala would have to be abandoned to the Gallas, it became necessary to provide for the safety of these volumes, which would otherwise have been destroyed by the Mohammedans. About 900 volumes were taken as far as Chelikot, and there about 600 were delivered to the priests of that church, one of the most important in Abyssinia; 359 books were retained for the purpose of scientific examination."

What makes it practically certain that this is a true report which has reached Europe is that a similar statement with regard to the existence of the books will be found in the Journals of the missionaries Isemberg and Krapf: we find in their account (p. 179) as follows:

"In the lake of Gurague called Suai five islands exist, in which the treasures of the ancient Abyssinian kings are said to have been hidden from Gragne [the Mohammedan desolator of Abyssinia] when he entered Abyssinia. That there are Ethiopic books is confirmed by a man whom the king sent as a spy."

In all probability, then, it is the books mentioned by Isemberg and Krapf that have been brought to light by king Menelek; and one can only hope that before long the contents of this newly-found library may be rendered accessible to Western scholars.

PRESBYTER GAIUS AND THE FOURTH GOSPEL.

(A Paper read before the Society for Historical Theology, November 28, 1895.)

THERE are some learned men whose works it is almost impossible to read with a proper degree of scepticism; their acquaintance with the subjects upon which they write is so wide, the considerations which they bring forward are so varied and new, the collateral information, both relevant and irrelevant, which they furnish is so stupendous, that the critical faculty becomes paralyzed in its most useful members, in its power to doubt and to contradict; and it is often only after long and weary study that we begin at last to realize that these great scholars were just as capable of running down a *cul de sac* as we are ourselves, and that we must resume with regard to them the habit of healthy distrust and apply it to many of their strongest and most elaborate demonstrations.

Such is the temper of mind in which I am trying to read Lightfoot, the writer of all others in our time whose criticisms seem to defy challenge and escape contradiction; and the object of the present paper is to shew in a brief, but I hope conclusive manner, the accumulation of errors for which Lightfoot is responsible in his treatment of a single problem of Church History, and the way in which our progress has been arrested by the erroneous hypothesis which he brought forward and his undue zeal in defending that hypothesis. I am referring to the question of Gaius the Presbyter, a famous third century writer, of whom Eusebius tells us that he wrote or held a dialogue against Proclus the Montanist in the days of Zephyrinus, and that he attacked in this dialogue the Chiliastic views which Cerinthus and others deduced from the Apocalypse, and probably attacked the Apocalypse itself.

As far back as 1868 in an article entitled '*Gaius or Hippolytus*,' published in the *Journal of Philology*, Lightfoot had maintained the theory that Gaius was merely the double of Hippolytus; and he brought forward a number of confirmatory considerations, which were revised and amplified in his *Apostolic Fathers*, a work in which, as I have intimated above, everything has the air of being final and infallible. These considerations were (i) that the historical allusions to Gaius agree exactly with parallel details in the life of Hippolytus; as, for instance, that they both flourished under Zephyrinus, that each was styled presbyter, that they both lived at Rome, that they were both learned men, that they both denied the Pauline authorship of the Epistle to the Hebrews, that each was antimontanistic, and that, more obscurely, the title 'Bishop of the Gentiles,' whatever it may mean, seems to have been applicable to either of them. And (ii) further than these historical allusions there were literary confusions between Gaius and Hippolytus of an extraordinary kind, which were made worse by the modern critics who insisted on referring every anonymous work of Hippolytus to the shadowy Gaius, until at last, as Lightfoot allowed, they overdid the matter by trying to make Gaius the author of the *Philosophumena*. Now since the *Philosophumena* is undoubtedly the work of Hippolytus, and the recognition of its authorship carries also the authorship of a number of lesser works which are in dispute, Gaius would have been a jay stripped of a mass of peacock's feathers and left to us merely as the author of the *Dialogue against Proclus the Montanist*, if it had not happened that Lightfoot ingeniously stuck all the feathers on again by maintaining that Gaius was Hippolytus, and that even the Dialogue against Proclus was due to the latter father. His explanation was that the title of the Dialogue in question ran as follows :

Διάλογος Γαΐου καὶ Πρόκλου
ἡ κατὰ Μοντανιστῶν,

and that Gaius is here either a literary lay-figure, which has given cause to a mass of subsequent misunderstandings, or that it is the actual prænomen of Hippolytus.

Now this was very ingenious; moreover it rid us of the troublesome and perplexing figure of the Higher Critic (for such Gaius

certainly was) in the Roman Church; it disposed of a person who
was of doubtful orthodoxy (for the fact that Gaius wrote against
the Montanists is not a set-off against his attack on the Johannine
writings; any stick is good enough to beat a Montanist dog), and
it left us a clearer view of the classic form of the great pupil of
Irenaeus, who seems to have never been guilty of anything worse
than Novatianism, and who in other respects was a genuine *malleus
haereticorum*. No doubt there is a certain advantage to be gained
from the fact that heretics turn to shades and their works do
follow them, while the orthodox defender of the Faith becomes
more and more imposing and real, so that we may say, with Homer,

$$\text{οἷος πέπνυται, τοὶ δὲ σκιαὶ ἀἴσσουσιν·}$$

in no other way could the rule 'quod semper, quod ubique, quod
ab omnibus' become verifiable. But, as it happens, in the case
which we are studying, the shade has evaded the Charon who had
ferried him over, and is back again, as in his last edition Lightfoot
admits, in the upper air.

The key to the problem, as in so many modern cases, is of
Syrian manufacture.

First of all, we are to set over against the fact of Gaius' attack
on the Apocalypse, and the statement on the back of the chair of
Hippolytus in the Lateran Museum that Hippolytus wrote a
treatise ὑπὲρ τοῦ κατὰ Ἰωάννην εὐαγγελίου καὶ ἀποκαλύψεως
the remarkable entry made by the Syriac writer Ebed-jesu at
the beginning of the 14th century that Hippolytus, Bishop and
Martyr, wrote a treatise called

ܪܫܝܐ ܕܠܘܩܒܠ ܓܐܝܘܣ

or 'Heads against Gaius.'

This latter entry ought to have been sufficient to prove that
Gaius was an antagonist of Hippolytus and not his double; and
taken with the first two statements to make it highly probable
that Gaius actually attacked both of the Johannine writings, for
the defence of Hippolytus is clearly a single work occupied with
the Johannine matter in the Canon. But, unfortunately, we have
not been in the habit of either studying or trusting Syriac writers
in the degree that they deserve.

The second direction from which the Syriac fathers come to
our aid is Dr Gwynn's discovery[1] that Dionysius Bar-Ṣalibi in his

[1] *Hermathena*, vol. vi. pp. 397—418.

Commentary upon the Apocalypse, of which a copy is extant in
the British Museum[1] (of course unpublished), quotes from the very
treatise referred to by Ebed-jesu, giving in a number of instances
the substance of the objections made by Gaius to the Apocalypse
and the replies of Hippolytus.

The recovery of these passages enabled Dr Gwynn to affirm
with certainty the separate identity of Gaius, and to prove that
Gaius had rejected the Apocalypse from the Canon on the ground
that it contained ' predictions mainly eschatological, irreconcilable
with the words of our Lord and the teaching of St Paul'; and
these views of Gaius were antagonized by Hippolytus in a treatise
whose title was probably ' Heads against Gaius', and we are thus
led to conjecture that the complete title was

Κεφάλαια κατὰ Γαΐου ὑπὲρ τοῦ κατὰ Ἰωάννην εὐαγγελίου
καὶ ἀποκαλύψεως,

or else that the work of Hippolytus existed also in an Epitome;
that is, we equate the title preserved in Syriac with the title on
the back of the chair, and so make Gaius to have attacked the
canonicity, not merely of the Apocalypse but also of the Fourth
Gospel. .

But here we are upon new ground, for we have taken a step
at which Dr Gwynn hesitated and drew back. For, finding
that in replying to Gaius, Hippolytus cites, once at least, from
St John's Gospel, he argues that this implies that Gaius accepted
the Fourth Gospel.   Indeed he says that it seems to follow *with
scarcely less certainty* than the preceding conclusions that *Gaius
accepted the Fourth Gospel as St John's.*   It is this statement into
the accuracy of which I propose to enquire.

But before doing so, it is instructive to recall some of the
obstacles through which we have threaded our way in the history
of the investigation.   Lightfoot in his last edition admitted the
weight of the new evidence brought forward by Dr Gwynn, but
suggested that, although Gaius may be come to life again, it may
be some other Gaius.   He clung to the theory which he had carefully elaborated, and was unwilling to abandon it.   I think this
tenacity is to be regretted; it would have been better to have
been more Saturnian with one's offspring.   But Lightfoot, of
course, granted at once that Gaius had written against the Apo-

calypse, and from this it follows that the remarks which Gaius makes about Cerinthus and the sensuous millennium which he proclaimed in the name of a great Apostle, must be understood as a criticism of the Apocalypse and the Chiliastic interpretations of it. In the light of which recently acquired knowledge it is interesting to compare the misunderstanding of the situation involved in the following sentence from Lightfoot (*Apost. Fathers*, Pt. I. vol. ii. p. 386), "It is difficult to see how an intelligent person should represent the Apocalypse as teaching that in the kingdom of Christ ' men should live in the flesh in Jerusalem and be the slaves of lusts and pleasures;' and again 'that a thousand years should be spent in marriage festivities.'" Amongst the people of ecclesiastical rank and dignity who held the view involved, though somewhat caricatured, in these words were Papias, Irenaeus, Nepos and Victorinus of Pettau. They certainly were not all of them idiots, though perhaps we may allow Papias the title of σφόδρα σμικρὸς τὸν νοῦν. The fact is that Lightfoot did not do justice to the Chiliastic movement.

Dr Gwynn is in the same case; in order to save the credit of the Apocalypse he ventures to suggest that Cerinthus "may have written a pseudo-Apocalypse, containing previsions of a millennium of carnal pleasures, and that Gaius, in his anti-millenarian over-zeal, may have rejected both Apocalypses, the genuine and the spurious alike." But since Cerinthus is credited with nothing worse than the rest of the Chiliastic succession, we have no reason to make him the author of a further Apocalypse, which would not also apply to the other fathers who are named, all of whom hold what their opponents call the 'sensuous millennium.' We must not multiply Apocalypses: the one which is certainly involved in the phenomena is sufficient for the explanation of the phenomena.

And now for our problem; did Gaius write against the Fourth Gospel, yea or nay?

The answer will come from the same quarter as before, for the Syrian Church holds the keys of all the problems. Suppose we turn to Dionysius Bar-Salibi's Commentary upon St John, of which a Latin translation is preserved in the Bodleian Library[1], made by Dudley Loftus from a MS. now in the Library of Trinity College, Dublin. We find the following sentence, which I give in Loftus' own words:

[1] *Fell MSS.* 6 and 7.

Gaius haereticus reprehendat Johannem quia non concors fuit cum sociis, dicentibus[1], quod post baptismum abiit in Galilaeam, et fecit miraculum vini in Kaṭna. *Sanctus Hypolitus e contrario* (l. adversus eum) scilicet, Christus postquam baptizatus fuerat, abiit in desertum, et quando inquisitio facta erat de illo per discipulos Johannis et per populum, quaerebant eum et non inveniebant eum, quia in deserto erat, cum vero finita fuisset tentatio et rediisset, venit in partes habitatas non ut baptizaretur, baptizatus enim jam fuerat, sed ut monstraretur a Johanne qui dixit intuens eum, ecce Agnus Dei! baptizatus igitur fuit et abiit in desertum dum exquirerent eum, et quod vidissent eum bene persuasi erant, quis fuit, sed quo abiisset non sciverant, sed quando rediisset persuasit eis ex quo quod monstratus fuit a Johanne, *crastino die vidit eum Johannes et dixit ecce agnus Dei!* istos quadraginta dies exquisiverunt eum et non viderunt eum; peractis vero diebus tentationis, cum venisset et visus esset venit in Galilaeam; quapropter inter se conveniunt Evangelistae quia postquam rediisset Dominus noster a deserto eumque monstrasset Johannes, illi, qui vidissent eum baptizatum, apprehendissent patrem clamautem, non viderunt eum amplius, quia abiit in desertum, necesse habuit Johannes ut iterum testimonium hujusmodi perhiberet de eo, quod hic est quam quaeritis *et illinc* abiit in Galilaeam virtute spiritus.

Now this extract at first sight seems to dispose completely of Dr Gwynn's statement as to the acceptance of the Fourth Gospel by Gaius. There is, however, a textual difficulty. On comparing Loftus' rendering with two MSS. in the British Museum (Codd. Add. 7184 and 12,143), I find reason to suspect that the name of Gaius was not in the primitive draft of the Commentary. For example the MS. Add. 7184 begins as follows:

ܐܝܢ ܙܝܪ ܐܝܘܡܐܒܝܐ ܡܢܐ ܘܝܐ ܗܘܐ ܩܘܐܢܦ

'A certain heretic had accused John &c.'

and a later hand adds above the line the word ܩܐܘܣ. On the other hand this addition is wholly wanting in the MS. Add. 12,143, and as we can see no reason for the omission of the name of Gaius in these two copies, we suspect that it has come in by editorial correction. Indeed the opening words which answer to the Greek αἱρετικός τις would of themselves suggest the absence

---

[1] We should probably correct the Syriac text and read *dicentem*.

of the name of the heretic. The question is whether the name is rightly added by way of identification. And to this I think we may answer in the affirmative; for the description of Hippolytus' reply which follows

ܕܩܕܝܫܐ ܐܦܘܠܝܛܘܣ ܠܘܩܒܠܗ

'Of the holy Hippolytus against him,'

immediately recalls the title 'Heads against Gaius.' And indeed there is no other candidate for the honour of the place of opposition. It is, moreover, interesting to compare the way in which the quotations are introduced with the passages quoted by Bar-Ṣalibi in his commentary on the Apocalypse.

The five cases given by Dr Gwynn are introduced as follows:

(i) ܓܐܝܘܣ ܐܪܣܝܘܛܐ ܕܠܘܩܒܠ ܗܢܐ ܓܠܝܢܐ
ܘܐܡܪ:

ܐܦܘܠܝܛܘܣ ܕܪܘܡܝ ܐܟܣܗ ܘܐܡܪ

i.e. 'Gaius the heretic, who objected to this Revelation and said ... Hippolytus of Rome refuted him and said'

(ii) ܓܐܝܘܣ ܐܡܪ:

ܘܐܡܪ ܐܦܘܠܝܛܘܣ ܠܘܩܒܠ ܗܕܐ ܗܦܟܬܐ
ܕܐܪܣܝܘܛܐ.

i.e. Gaius said:
and Hippolytus said in reply to this objection of the heretic:

(iii) ܗܪܟܐ ܡܥܩܒ ܓܐܝܘܣ:

ܘܐܦܘܠܝܛܘܣ ܡܟܣ ܠܗ ܘܐܡܪ

i.e. Here Gaius objected...
and Hippolytus refuted him and said:

(iv) ܓܐܝܘܣ:

ܐܦܘܠܝܛܘܣ ܠܘܩܒܠܗ.

i.e. Gaius:
Hippolytus against him...

(v) ܓܐܝܘܣ ܗܐܪܛܝܩܐ ܐܥܩܒ:

ܐܦܘܠܝܛܘܣ ܐܟܣܗ ܠܗܢܐ ܘܐܡܪ:

i.e. Gaius the heretic objected...
Hippolytus refuted this and said.

and these prefaces are so closely parallel to the passage which we
have quoted from Bar-Ṣalibi's Commentary on the Fourth Gospel,
that we need have no hesitation in saying that if the name of
Gaius was wanting in the first copy, it has been rightly suggested
by later readers. And if this be so, we can only regard as a
serious misstatement Dr Gwynn's remark that it follows with
hardly less certainty than the fact that Gaius lived and opposed
the canonicity of the Apocalypse that the said Gaius accepted the
Fourth Gospel.

But in order that the matter should be put outside of doubt,
we will take the argument a little further and examine what
Epiphanius brings forward in his treatment of the 51st Heresy,
that of the people whom he calls the *Alogi*. It is commonly
supposed that this title is an invention of Epiphanius to describe
the people who did not believe in the Johannine writings, which
contain the Doctrine of the Logos. And Epiphanius actually says
in c. 3 Τί φάσκουσιν τοίνυν οἱ Ἄλογοι; Ταύτην γὰρ αὐτοῖς
τίθημι τὴν ἐπωνυμίαν· ἀπὸ γὰρ τῆς δεῦρο οὕτως κληθήσονται, καὶ
οὕτως, ἀγαπητοί, ἐπιθῶμεν αὐτοῖς ὄνομα, τουτέστιν Ἄλογοι. And
he speaks with the same air of originality in c. 28, in the words,
Ἠλέγχθησαν καὶ οἱ ἀποβαλλόμενοι τὸ κατὰ Ἰωάννην εὐαγγέλιον,
οὓς δικαίως Ἀλόγους καλέσομαι, ἐπειδὴ τὸν λόγον τοῦ θεοῦ ἀπο-
βάλλονται, τὸν διὰ Ἰωάννην κηρυχθέντα κτέ. There is, however,
a curious feature in the title of the refutation of this heresy which
suggests that this originality is an illusion. For the title runs as
follows: Κατὰ τῆς αἱρέσεως τῆς μὴ δεχομένης τὸ κατὰ Ἰωάννην
εὐαγγέλιον καὶ τὴν Ἀποκάλυψιν, ἣν ἐκάλεσεν Ἀνοήτων, τρια-
κοστὴ πρώτη, ἡ καὶ πεντηκοστὴ πρώτη. Here the obvious
suggestion is to restore Ἀλόγων for Ἀνοήτων in harmony with
the passages quoted above. But how did the error arise? The
answer is, I think, as follows: the title must have been confused
with the title of another heresy, viz. the heresy of Noetus, to
whom the appellation of Ἀνόητος would be peculiarly applicable.
And when we turn to the heresy in question, which is the 57th in
Epiphanius' list, we find him using this very play upon the name,
though it does not appear in the title prefixed to the heresy. For
example in c. 4 he says καὶ διέπεσεν ἐκ πανταχόθεν ὁ τῆς
ἀνοησίας σου λόγος, ὦ ἀνόητε. It is to this heresy then that
the name applies. We may also compare c. 6 οὗτος καὶ ὁ ἀπ'
αὐτοῦ Νοητοῦ ἔχων ὄνομα ἀνόητος ὑπάρχει καὶ οἱ ἐξ αὐτοῦ ἀνοη-

τοῦντες, also c. 8 Τί οὖν ἐρεῖ Νοητὸς ἐν τῇ αὐτοῦ ἀνοησίᾳ; etc. etc. Now when we turn to the heresy of the Noetians as described by Philaster (Haer. 53) we find that the same play upon words occurs, as the following sentence will shew:

alii autem Noetiani *insensati* cuiusdam nomine Noëti, qui dicebat patrem omnipotentem ipsum esse Christum;

and here, as Lipsius shews, the word *insensati* stands for ἀνοήτου. And a comparison with the language of Hippolytus *contra Noetum* shews that Philaster is following Hippolytus closely; so that we reasonably infer that the play upon the name began originally with Hippolytus, and this inference is fully confirmed by an examination of Hippolytus' treatment of the subject. For not only does Hippolytus shew an acquaintance with the joke, but we can see the way in which he was led to it. He compares the theological system of Noetus with that of Heraclitus, in which all contraries are harmonized so that crooked things are the same as straight things, mortal and immortal are equivalent terms, and God is at once 'summer and winter, peace and war, satiety and famine.' What wonder then if he should apply the same reasoning to the name of Noetus, who should turn out to be Anoetus! And that he does so reason will appear from *Ref. Haer.* ix. 10, where he follows the sentence Ὁ θεὸς...πόλεμος, εἰρήνη, κόρος, λιμός by saying Τἀναντία ἅπαντα. οὗτος (*l.* οὕτως) ὁ νοῦς.... Φανερὸν δὲ πᾶσι τοὺς νοητοὺς (*l.* ἀνοήτους) Νοητοῦ διαδόχους καὶ τῆς αἰρέσεως προστάτας, εἰ καὶ Ἡρακλείτου λέγοισαν ἑαυτοὺς μὴ γεγονέναι ἀκροατάς, ἀλλά γε τὰ τῷ Νοητῷ δόξαντα αἱρουμένους ἀναφανδὸν, ταῦτα ὁμολογεῖν. For, as he continues, they hold the doctrine of contraries in regard to the Divine Nature. It was reasonable, then, that they should furnish a parallel to it in themselves.

But if this title is derived primarily from the wit of Hippolytus it is not unreasonable to suppose that the title Ἄλογος which it has displaced in the text of Epiphanius comes from the same mint. For Epiphanius does not, apparently, use the title Ἀνόητοι at the head of his treatment of the heresy of Noetus, however much it is involved in the text: yet it must have stood in the list of heresies, in order that a transcriptional confusion should arise between the *Alogi* and the *Anoeti*. We infer, therefore, that the presence of the title *Alogi* is probable in the book or table of

4—2

heresies upon which Epiphanius is working. And with this
Lightfoot agrees (*S. Clement of Rome*, ii. 394), for he says, "We
may suspect that Epiphanius borrowed the name ἄλογοι, 'the
irrational ones,' from Hippolytus; for these jokes are very much
in his way; e.g. νοητός, ἀνόητος, and δοκός, δοκεῖν, δοκηταί." We
may also add the heresy which Epiphanius describes as Κηριν-
θιανοὶ ἤτοι Μηρινθιανοί[1] to our list,· and here Epiphanius has
failed to see the Hippolytean joke (Μήρινθος = a noose) and
discusses whether it is one person or two that is meant.

So much for the title of the 51st Heresy: it suggests the use
of Hippolytean material; and now let us turn to the text of the
section. It is mainly made up of two separable defences, that of
the Fourth Gospel and that of the Apocalypse. For aught
Epiphanius knows (τάχα), the Alogi may have also rejected the
Johannine Epistles which confirm the authenticity of the other
two books, but he is concerned only with material furnished by
the attacks upon the greater Johannine writings. He deals
accordingly with selected objections. And amongst the refutations
which he makes of the attacks on the Apocalypse there is, as
Dr Gwynn has pointed out, one which is closely parallel to one of
the instances in the Bar-Salibi extracts from the Heads against
Gaius. For convenience we will print the text of Epiphanius side
by side with the Gwynn-Gaius fragment:

Epiph. Haer. li. c. 34.

καί φασιν ὅτι, Εἶδον, καὶ εἶπε τῷ ἀγγέλῳ,
Λῦσον τοὺς τέσσαρας ἀγγέλους τοὺς ἐπὶ τοῦ
Εὐφράτου· καὶ ἤκουσα τὸν ἀριθμὸν τοῦ στρατοῦ,
μύριαι μυριάδες καὶ χίλιαι χιλιάδες, καὶ ἦσαν
ἐνδεδυμένοι θώρακας πυρίνους καὶ θειώδεις καὶ
ὑακινθίνους. Ἐνόμισαν γὰρ οἱ τοιοῦτοι, μή πη
ἄρα γελοῖόν ἐστιν ἡ ἀλήθεια· ἐὰν γὰρ λέγῃ τοὺς
τέσσαρας ἀγγέλους τοὺς ἐν τῷ Εὐφράτῃ καθεζομένους, ἵνα δείξῃ τὰς τέσσαρας διαφορὰς τῶν
ἐκεῖσε ἐθνῶν καθεζομένων ἐπὶ τὸν Εὐφράτην,
οἵτινές εἰσιν Ἀσσύριοι, Βαβυλώνιοι, Μῆδοι καὶ
Πέρσαι. Αὗται γὰρ αἱ τέσσαρες βασιλεῖαι κατὰ
διαδοχὴν ἐν τῷ Δανιὴλ ἐμφέρονται, ὡς πρῶτοι
Ἀσσύριοι ἐβασίλευον, καὶ Βαβυλώνιοι ἐν χρόνοις
αὐτοῦ, Μῆδοι δὲ διεδέξαντο, μετ' αὐτοὺς δὲ
Πέρσαι, ὧν πρῶτος γέγονε Κῦρος ὁ βασιλεύς.
Τὰ γὰρ ἔθνη ὑπὸ ἀγγέλους τεταγμένα εἰσίν, ὡς

Gaius.

*And the angels were loosed,
which were prepared for sea-
sons and for days to slay the
third part of men* (Rev. ix.
15). On this Caius says:
It is not written that angels
are to make war, nor that a
third part of men is to
perish: but that *nation shall
rise against nation* (Matt.
xxiv. 7). Hippolytus in reply to him: It is not of
angels he says they are to go
to war, but that four nations
are to arise out of the region
which is *by Euphrates* and to
come against the earth and

[1] See Lightfoot, *Lectures on St John.*

ἐπιμαρτυρεῖ μοι Μωϋσῆς ὁ ἅγιος τοῦ Θεοῦ θεράπων, τὸν λόγον κατὰ ἀκολουθίαν ἑρμηνεύων καὶ λέγων, Ἐπερώτησον τὸν πατέρα σου καὶ ἀγγελεῖ σοι, τοὺς πρεσβυτέρους καὶ ἐροῦσί σοι· Ὅτε διεμέριζεν ὁ ὕψιστος ἔθνη, ὡς διέσπειρεν υἱοὺς Ἀδάμ, ἔστησεν ὅρια ἐθνῶν κατὰ ἀριθμὸν ἀγγέλων Θεοῦ· καὶ ἐγενήθη μερὶς κυρίου λαὸς αὐτοῦ Ἰακώβ, σχοίνισμα κληρονομίας αὐτοῦ Ἰσραήλ. Εἰ οὖν τὰ ἔθνη ὑπὸ ἀγγέλους εἰσὶ τεταγμένα, δικαίως εἶπε, Λῦσον τοὺς τέσσαρας ἀγγέλους τοὺς ἐν τῷ Εὐφράτῃ καθεζομένους καὶ ἐπεχομένους ἐπιτρέπειν τοῖς ἔθνεσιν εἰς πόλεμον, ἕως καιροῦ μακροθυμίας κυρίου, ἕως προστάξει δι' αὐτῶν ἐκδικίαν γενέσθαι τῶν αὐτοῦ ἁγίων. Ἐκρατοῦντο γὰρ οἱ ἐπιτεταγμένοι ἄγγελοι ὑπὸ τοῦ πνεύματος μὴ ἔχοντες καιρὸν ἐπιδρομῆς, διὰ τὸ μήπω λύεω αὐτοῖς τὴν δίκην, τοῦ τὰ λοιπὰ ἔθνη λύεσθαι ἕνεκεν τῆς πρὸς τοὺς ἁγίους ὕβρεως. Λύονται δὲ οἱ τοιοῦτοι καὶ ἐπέρχονται τῇ γῇ ὡς Ἰωάννης προφητεύει καὶ οἱ λοιποὶ προφῆται. Καὶ γὰρ κινούμενοι οἱ ἄγγελοι κινοῦσι τὰ ἔθνη εἰς ὁρμὴν ἐκδικίας. Ὅτι δὲ πυρίνους καὶ θειώδεις καὶ ὑακινθίνους θώρακας σημαίνει, οὐδεὶς ἀμφιβάλλει. Ἐκεῖνα γὰρ τὰ ἔθνη ἀπὸ τῆς τοιαύτης χρόας ἔχει τὴν ἀμφίασιν. Τὰ μὲν γὰρ θειώδη ἱμάτια χρόα τίς ἐστι μηλίνη οὕτω καλουμένη ἐρέα. τὰ δὲ πύρινα, ἵνα εἴπῃ τὰ κοκκηρὰ ἐνδύματα, καὶ ὑακίνθινα, ἵνα δείξῃ τὴν καλλαΐνην ἐρέαν.

to war with mankind. But this that he says, *four angels* is not alien from Scripture. Moses said, *When He dispersed the sons of Adam, He set the boundary of the nations according to the number of the angels of God* (Deut. xxxii. 8). Since therefore nations have been assigned to angels, and each nation pertains to one angel, John rightly declared by the Revelation a loosing for those four angels : who are the Persians and the Medes and the Babylonians and the Assyrians. Since then those angels who have been appointed over the nations have not been commanded to stir up those who have been assigned to them, a certain bond of the power of the word is indicated which restrains them until the day shall arrive and the Lord of all shall command. And this then is to happen when Antichrist shall come.

The parallelism between the two lines of defence is so striking that it betrays a common origin, and this must be the work of Hippolytus, which has been rehandled by Epiphanius, and which appears, perhaps in an abbreviated form, in the extracts of Bar-Salibi. Such an abbreviation might be due to Bar-Salibi himself, or to the fact that the *Heads against Gaius* is a summary of a larger work.

But if this be the case, that we are dealing with lost Hippolytean and Gaian matter, we cannot limit ourselves to the single passage in which Epiphanius and Bar-Salibi agree. We must group together all the extracts in the two writers which defend the Apocalypse, and regard them as the residue of a single lost work; after which we must make a similar investigation with regard to the Fourth Gospel.

We thus learn, over and above what Bar-Salibi tells us, that

the Alogi objected to the machinery of the Apocalypse, especially
to the Angels and Trumpets; and that they criticised the Epistle
to Thyatira, on the ground that no Church existed in Thyatira in
St John's day.

And the same method of enquiry holds with regard to the
relation of Gaius to the Fourth Gospel: for we find Epiphanius
dealing with a series of objections made to the Chronology of the
Fourth Gospel and to special disagreements between St John and
the Synoptics, and we shall see that under both·these heads he is
dealing with Hippolytean matter; the replies are the replies of
Hippolytus, rehandled by Epiphanius, and the Chronology is the
Hippolytean modification of the work of Julius Africanus.

We have shewn from Bar-Ṣalibi a single instance of a Gaian
objection to the Fourth Gospel, viz. the discordant accounts of the
events connected with the Baptism. And when we turn to
Epiphanius we find that the very first objection of the Alogi
which he refutes is this very difficulty. Φάσκουσι γὰρ καθ'
ἑαυτῶν, οὐ γὰρ εἴποιμι κατὰ τῆς ἀληθείας, ὅτι οὐ συμφωνεῖ τὰ
αὐτοῦ βιβλία τοῖς λοιποῖς ἀποστόλοις. Here Epiphanius is
working on a text which read ἑτέροις for which he gives λοιποῖς;
for we find the equivalent sentence in Bar-Ṣalibi:

quia non concors fuit cum sociis (i.e. ἑταίροις).

The form of the objection turns upon the quotation of a
number of verses from the beginning of the Gospel, such as:
Ὁ Ἰωάννης μαρτυρεῖ, καὶ κέκραγε, λέγων ὅτι, οὗτός ἐστιν ὃν
εἶπον ὑμῖν· καὶ ὅτι, Οὗτός ἐστιν ὁ ἀμνὸς τοῦ θεοῦ, ὁ αἴρων τὴν
ἁμαρτίαν τοῦ κόσμου· καὶ καθεξῆς φησι, Καὶ εἶπον αὐτῷ οἱ
ἀκούσαντες, Ῥαββὶ, ποῦ μενεῖς; ἅμα δὲ ἐν ταὐτῷ, Τῇ ἐπαύριον,
φησὶν, ἠθέλησεν ἐξελθεῖν εἰς τὴν Γαλιλαίαν καὶ εὑρίσκει Φίλιππον,
καὶ λέγει αὐτῷ ὁ Ἰησοῦς, Ἀκολούθει μοι. Καὶ μετὰ τοῦτο ὀλίγῳ
πρόσθεν φησὶ, Καὶ μετὰ τρεῖς ἡμέρας γάμος ἐγένετο ἐν Κανᾷ τῆς
Γαλιλαίας κτέ.

Epiphanius' reply is long and diffuse; he begins by pointing
out that the same method of criticism might be applied to· the
internal disagreements of the Synoptics; how, for example, are
we to piece together the infancy accounts in Matthew and Luke;
and how are we to place the visit of the Magi and the flight into
Egypt, so as to be in harmony with the presentation of Christ
in the Temple etc. The criticism of the Alogi who accepted the

Synoptics could thus be easily directed against themselves. When at length Epiphanius comes to the discussion of the Johannine passage, he explains that the Lord, after his baptism, went into the wilderness, returned to Nazareth, and afterwards came back again to the Jordan where John was baptizing : ἵνα δείξῃ μετὰ τὰς τεσσαράκοντα ἡμέρας τοῦ πειρασμοῦ, καὶ μετὰ τὴν ἀπ' αὐτοῦ τοῦ πειρασμοῦ ἐπάνοδον καὶ ὁρμὴν τὴν ἐπὶ Ναζαρὲτ καὶ Γαλιλαίαν, ὡς οἱ ἄλλοι τρεῖς εὐαγγελισταὶ ἔφησαν, πάλιν ἐπὶ τὸν Ἰορδάνην αὐτὸν ἡκέναι κτέ.

And this is substantially the same as we find in the passage in Bar-Ṣalibi, so that we may claim again the recognition of Hippolytean matter.

The second difficulty which he undertakes to handle is the question of the number of passovers in our Lord's ministry. According to the Alogi, John mentions two passovers in our Lord's ministry, the Synoptics only one. Epiphanius adds the accounts together and argues, reasonably enough, for three passovers. But he is evidently falling foul of the belief of the early Church that our Lord's ministry was confined to a single year, an opinion which was based upon or confirmed by the words of Isaiah that he came to preach *the acceptable year of the Lord*. Accordingly Epiphanius, who is working at the data of some Chronographer, that our Lord was born on the 11th of the Egyptian month Tybi, and that he was baptized in his 30th year on the 12th of the Egyptian month Athyr proceeds to the question of the acceptable year in the following words ; καὶ ἀπεντεῦθεν ἀπὸ Ἀθὺρ δωδεκάτης κηρύττοντος αὐτοῦ τὸν δεκτὸν ἐνιαυτὸν κυρίου κτέ. And certainly he argues, the Lord did preach the acceptable year, because for the first year of his ministry he met with general acceptance, but after that with opposition! This ingenious argument shews that Epiphanius is trying to get rid of the theory of a single year of the ministry, which he found in his sources.

Now it would be very interesting if we could compare the Chronology which Epiphanius gives with that of Hippolytus either as it existed in the *Chronica* or as we are entitled to assume that it must have existed in the defence of the Fourth Gospel and the Apocalypse (for certainly Hippolytus must have dealt with the objection made by the Alogi on the subject of the Passovers).

But unfortunately we are dealing here with lost documents. What does seem clear is that Epiphanius has been tinkering the data before him; for he alters the date of Christ's death, which in the Hippolytean tradition is usually the consulate of the two Gemini, and makes it two years later, by assuming in the life of our Lord two further consulates, of which the first is that of Rufus (Fufius) and Rubellio (*who are in fact the Gemini over again*); and the second is the consulate of Vinicius and Longinus Cassius. It is clear that such a confusion as this cannot be due to Hippolytus, and we suspect that some one has been trying to add a couple of years to the tale.

But in the next place when we compare the list of consuls given by Epiphanius for the first thirty years of our Lord's life with the table in the Chronographer of 354 which is taken from the Hippolytean table of 234, we find that Epiphanius has placed the birth of Christ two consulates earlier than the Chronographer; and this again suggests an attempt to gain two years in our Lord's life by some one who was working on a chronicle of 31 years which he was trying to turn into one of 33 years. Now whether all of this confusion is due to Epiphanius, or whether part of it is due to Hippolytus who has emended the 31 year life of Christ which appears in his paschal cycle into some system more consistent with the Gospels, I am not at present prepared to say; it is possible that the correction is due to more than a single reformer.

At all events, we may be confident that Hippolytus in dealing with Gaius must have had to face the difficulty of the Chronology, and if he did not succeed in abandoning the theory of the acceptable year, Epiphanius must have done it for him, and done it with much blundering. But behind all these confused data of Epiphanius there must lie the Hippolytean tables as they were taken from Africanus. And perhaps some day we may be able to say how much of the work of Africanus has escaped mutilation at the hands of those who worked him over. We have shown, then, that Epiphanius in his 51st heresy, that of the Alogi, is using material which was taken in part at least from the reply of Hippolytus to Gaius in defence of the fourth Gospel and the Apocalypse. And it is clear, since Hippolytus would not have been defending what no one was attacking, that objections were still current at Rome in the early part of the third century to the canonicity of the fourth Gospel. How much is involved in this admission as regards the existence of a previous succession of adverse Higher Critics, is difficult to say. In the case of the Apocalypse the objection taken can easily be seen to be early and constant and widely diffused. Whether criticism of the same intensity was applied to the fourth Gospel, we have no means of determining: but it is a fixed point gained to have restored, as Dr Gwynn has done, the personality of Gaius : and to have defined, as we hope to have done, his position as a critic.

AN EXTRACT FROM THE COMMENTARY OF DIONYSIUS BAR-SALIBI ON THE GOSPEL OF JOHN (c. ii. v. 1).

From (A) Cod. Mus. Britt. Add. 7184, f. 2432 with some variants
from (B) Cod. Mus. Britt. Add. 12,143.

[Syriac text, 12 lines — body of the extract, with footnote reference markers [1], [2], [3]]

---

[1] A (not B) adds on marg. in a late hand:

[Syriac text]

[2] A (not B) adds on marg. in a late hand : [Syriac text]

[3] A (not B) adds over line in a late hand [Syriac text]

ܡܫܝܚܐ ܒܬܪ ܕܥܡܕ ܢܦܩ ܠܡܕܒܪܐ. ܘܟܕ ܗܘܬ
ܟܠܬܐ ܡܬܠܠܬܗ ܡܢ ܬܠܡܝܕܘܗܝ ܕܝܘܚܢ ܘܡܢ ܟܡܐ
ܘܒܬܒܝܢ ܗܘܘ ܠܗ ܠܐ ܐܫܬܘܕܥܘܗܝ. ܒܗܝ ܕܒܡܕܒܪܐ
ܗܘܐ. ܟܕ ܕܝܢ ܥܒܠ ܠܡܫܘܐ ܘܗܦܟ ܐܬܐ ܠܓܠܝܠܐ
ܠܗ ܕܢܥܒܕ. ܒܥܒܕ ܗܘܐ ܚܡܪ. ܐܠܐ ܕܢܬܚܘܐ ܡܢ
ܢܘܫܢ. ܠܗܘ ܕܟܕ ܫܘܝܗܝ ܐܡܪ. ܕܗܘܐ ܐܡܪܗ ܕܐܠܗܐ.
ܡܕܝܢ ܒܬܪ ܘܐܙܠ ܠܡܕܒܪܐ ܟܕ ܡܟܡܟܝܢ ܗܘܘ ܟܠܗܘܢ.
ܘܕܫܐܘܗܝ ܡܩܦܝܢ ܗܘܘ. ܗܝ ܕܡܢ ܐܬܦܘܗܝ ܗܘܐ.
ܘܠܐܡܕܐ ܐܙܠ ܠܐ ܫܕܝܢ ܗܘܘ. ܘܟܕ ܗܦܟ ܐܦܫ
ܐܢܘܢ. ܒܬܪ ܕܐܬܦܘܗܝ ܡܢ ܢܘܫܢ. ܠܢܘܡܐ ܕܡܫܪ
ܫܘܝܗܝ ܢܘܫܢ ܘܐܡܪ. ܗܘ ܐܡܪܗ ܕܐܠܗܐ. ܒܗܠܝܢ
ܐܪܟܝܢ ܢܘܡܢ ܒܒܐܘܗܝ ܘܠܐ ܫܐܘܗܝ. ܘܒܬܪ ܗܠܝܢ
ܕܢܘܫܐ ܟܕ ܐܬܐ ܘܐܬܚܝܝ ܐܬܐ ܠܓܠܝܠܐ. ܡܕܝܢ
ܥܒܠܝܢ ܐܘܢܓܠܝܣܛܐ ܠܫܢܝܐ. ܡܛܠ ܕܒܬܪ ܕܗܦܟ
ܡܢ ܡܕܒܪܐ. ܘܫܢܗ ܢܘܫܢ ܠܗܘܢ ܕܫܘ
ܕܒܬܪ ܘܠܐܡܕܐ ܕܥܒܕܐ ܘܠܐ ܫܐܘܗܝ ܬܘܒ. ܡܛܠ
ܕܟܠ ܠܡܕܒܪܐ. ܐܫܬܢܝ ܢܘܫܢ ܕܢܫܡܥ ܟܠܗܘܢ
ܬܫܥܝܬ: ܒܗܝ ܕܗܢܘ ܕܒܚܝܢ ܐܢܬܘܢ. ܘܡܢ ܬܡܢ ܐܙܠ
ܠܓܠܝܠܐ ܒܫܠܝܐ ܕܝܘܡܐ

EUTHALIUS AND EUSEBIUS.

By the publication of his researches into the problems associated with the name of Euthalius of Alexandria, Prof. Robinson has laid all New Testament scholars under a great debt of gratitude. If his *Euthaliana* had done nothing more than restore to us a number of pages of the famous Codex H of the Pauline Epistles by the simple process of reading the impress of the ink of the perished pages upon the pages which remain, it would have been a distinct paleographical triumph. For it must be remembered that this MS. of which the extant leaves are scattered over the libraries of Paris, St Petersburg, Moscow, Kieff, Turin and Mt Athos, has been the object of study of a great many pairs of eyes that are usually in the habit of seeing. Dr Gregory, acting as literary executor to Tischendorf, had certainly planned an edition of the H-fragments, and made preparation for that edition, yet he does not seem to have suspected that the worn and stained pages had a double tale to tell, and could furnish the text of leaves lost as well as of leaves preserved. We also made a careful study of this Codex, so far as its Paris fragments are concerned, yet it never dawned upon our minds that the set-off on the pages belonged to a different set of pages than those which were extant; nor did the thought occur to us when, not long since, we were examining the Athos fragments. These Athos leaves were also examined by Duchesne[1], but neither does he appear to have suspected that there was any supplementary evidence forthcoming from the manuscript.

More curious still, M. Omont in publishing an edition of the St Petersburg leaves, actually read a lost page of the MS. by the

---

[1] *Archives des Missions scientifiques et littéraires*, ser. 3, vol. 3. Paris, 1876.

reversed writing, but does not seem to have applied his method to any further leaves either at Paris or St Petersburg. It is, therefore, a distinct triumph and a very welcome increase to our knowledge that Prof. Robinson, working independent of us all, has been able to read, without serious lacunae, sixteen fresh pages of this valuable text.

But, valuable as this increment to our knowledge is, it is only a small part of Mr Robinson's services to the critic who occupies himself with the supposed Euthalian text of the Epistles and the shadowy editor of that text. He has passed under review almost the whole of the literature of the subject from Zacagni onwards, with the view of determining all that can be known with regard to the person and work of Euthalius. And in so doing he has shewn a remarkable grasp of critical methods, far beyond what one is used to look for in English work. Nor is the study the less interesting because the author displays such evident delight in knocking down all the ninepins which recent students of Euthalius had set up, including Ehrhard, Dobschütz, Conybeare and myself. 'The scholar's melancholy,' as Shakespeare says, 'is emulation.' We have sometimes a touch of the complaint ourselves, and Prof. Robinson will not be angry if we indulge the hope that, as far as our own ninepins are concerned, we may be able to set some of them up again. At least that is the object of the following pages. But whether we succeed in our attempt or not, we have a good hope that we shall not leave the subject without adding to our knowledge something which will be of permanent value.

This is the third time, I think, that I have approached the Euthalian problems. The first occasion was when in connexion with the study of the Stichometry of ancient MSS. I came across the collection of Euthalian and Ps.-Euthalian data which Zacagni had amassed in his *Collectanea Monumentorum Veterum*, and undertook to prove, as against the traditional view held by Scholz, Scrivener and others, that the lines numbered by Euthalius were not sense-lines (*cola* and *commata* as they are sometimes called) but space-lines of which the unit of measurement is a 16-syllabled hexameter. There has been no exception taken to this demonstration (nor is it easy to see how any exception was possible, for the investigation was self-verifying); but a new point has been raised by Prof. Robinson who questions with great propriety why we should attribute to Euthalius at once the art of writing the

N.T. in sense-lines, and the counting of the N.T. and attached
matter in space-lines. He proposes, therefore, to divide the
Euthalian materials, speaking roughly, between two artists of
whom one, Euthalius, should write the Acts and Epistles in *cola*,
and add certain prologues, while the other, whom he identifies
with an Evagrius who appears in the subscription to certain
Euthalian MSS. (notably in Cod. H, as recent investigations have
shewn) should publish an *editio minor* of the Euthalian text and
materials and be responsible for the stichometry, properly so
called, of the text and prologues. This suggestion has a great air
of probability about it. For the present we leave it on one side,
as we hope to re-open the investigation from a fresh quarter.
Most of what we had said upon the interpretation of the
Euthalian lines will be found reprinted in the little volume
Stichometry[1].

The second attack which we made upon the Euthalian problem
dealt with the obscure personalities of the writer and of the person
to whom the work was dedicated. It is well known that there is
a great air of uncertainty about the titles prefixed to the works
attributed to Euthalius. The MSS. speak, but by no means
uniformly, of Euthalius of Sulci, but no one knows where Sulci
is, not even Prof. Robinson, for it is almost impossible to refer
the work to Sardinia, where a place of that name is known ; they
make Euthalius a bishop, but we cannot identify either him or his
diocese. His first work, that on the Pauline Epistles, is based
upon the previous work of a pious father whom he does not name,
though he speaks of him flatteringly enough, and the influence
has not been an unnatural one that the father in question was not
exactly in the very odour of sanctity; and internal evidence has
been produced which suggested that the great nameless one might
perhaps be Theodore of Mopsuestia. In the second part of his
work, that which deals with the Acts and the Catholic Epistles,
Euthalius (whoever he was) expressly addresses in his prologues a
father of the name of Athanasius; but here, too, the critic found a
difficulty, for of the actual dates found in the Euthalian prefaces
one (A.D. 396) was too late for Athanasius the Great, and the other
(A.D. 458), which might seem to refer the work to the time of the
second Athanasius, appeared not to be due to the hand of the
original author of the Prologues.

---

[1] *Stichometry*, Cambridge University Press Warehouse, 1893.

At this point I took up the matter with the object of proving that the name of Athanasius which occurs in the Prologues to the Acts and Catholic Epistles is an orthodox substitute for an unorthodox name which has disappeared; and, guided by what seemed to me an obvious and repeated play upon words in the Euthalian text, where there were frequent and significant allusions to Μελέτη or study, I maintained that the work was originally dedicated to a father of the name of Meletius upon whose name Euthalius was playing, and that its true title was Εὐθαλίου πρὸς Μελέτιον.

The subordinate question, as to which of the possible Meletii of doubtful ecclesiastical repute was the one to whom the book was dedicated was decided, perhaps too rapidly, in favour of Meletius of Mopsuestia, the pupil and successor of the great Theodore. In making this identification, I was, of course, influenced by the first of the two dates (A.D. 396) found amongst the Euthalian matter, which I took to be the true date of Euthalius.

But to all this Prof. Robinson takes exception: according to him the date 396 is not the date of Euthalius, but of his successor Evagrius, and consequently we have no chronological difficulty to get over in accepting the ascription of certain MSS. and of the text itself to Athanasius; while, as to the supposed play upon a name, while not entirely denying that there is something of the kind involved, he thinks that it is merely a play upon a word capable of two senses, because Μελέτη, which I take to be the key-word to the understanding of the prologues, is a word which may mean either *study* or *training* in the athletic sense: according to which interpretation, since the word *training* is susceptible of a double sense even amongst ourselves, we are to understand Euthalius as saying 'I recommend to you my foster-sister and friend, the appropriately named lady, Madam Training.' And Prof. Robinson concludes by saying, 'I cannot myself think that a case is made out for any deletion of the name Meletius at all.' With which observation he finally knocked over my ninepin!

Now, as far as I am concerned, I have no special objection to be put in the wrong, but inasmuch as we are obliged by Euthalius to sing the praises of Mistress Study, whoever she was, and the praise ought not to be mere superficial adulation, it might be as well to make the examination a little more closely concerning these

two points, the question of the supposed Meletius whom I maintain
to have been erased, and the subordinate issue as to the date of
Euthalius. The latter question can, indeed, be treated indepen-
dently of the former; for, as Mr Robinson allows, if A.D. 396 is
the date of Evagrius and not of Euthalius, there is at least one
other Meletius of an earlier date, viz. Meletius of Antioch, who
might be a candidate at once for ecclesiastical disgrace and the
hand of Melete; but I shall not abandon the date 396 for Euthalius without applying to the subject some more of the sleepless
discipline which Euthalius praises; and as for Melete, who has
engaged me as well as the pious father of antiquity in her toils, if
I find her fallacious, she shall be burnt for a witch.

And so we come to our third contribution to the Euthalian
problem, which is *the relation of the prologues of Euthalius to the
text of Eusebius.* According to Robinson (and the impression is
not an unnatural one), Euthalius is a very original writer, with a
'great wealth of expression,' a person who can not only talk in
high-sounding Greek, but who would also not sully his style by
'repeating his own language in a slavish manner': in other words
a literary artist of some eminence whose commodity of words and
of ideas (which words are meant either to express or to conceal) is
something more than

　　　　A beggarly array of empty boxes,
　　　Of musty packthread and old cakes of roses.

I will confess that, until recently, I shared with Mr Robinson
this idea of Euthalius; he was one of the writers who drove one
to the dictionary, and such we always respect—and hate. But I
hope to be able to shew that this grandeur of style is only
apparent, and that, in reality, one of the main uses of the swollen
speech of Euthalius is to furnish various readings for the text of
Eusebius!

In the first place, then, we observe that Euthalius himself has
directed us to Eusebius as one of his sources: he tells us, in his
Prologue to the Pauline Epistles (Zacagni, p. 531) as follows:

Εὐσέβιος δὲ, τοὺς μετέπειτα χρόνους ἀκριβῶς περιεργασάμενος,
ἱστόρησεν ἡμῖν καὶ ἐν τῷ δευτέρῳ τόμῳ τῆς Ἐκκλησιαστικῆς
ἱστορίας τούτου καὶ τὸ μαρτύριον· καί φησι τὸν Παῦλον ἄνετον
διατρίψαι καὶ τὸν τοῦ Θεοῦ λόγον ἀκωλύτως κηρύξαι ἐπισημηνάμενος. Τότε μὲν οὖν ἐπὶ Νέρωνος ἀπολογησάμενον τὸν Παῦλον
αὖθις ἐπὶ τὴν τοῦ κηρύγματος διακονίαν λόγος ἔχει στείλασθαι.

The passage, to which we shall presently have to refer more at length, is taken from Euseb. *H. E.* ii. 22, where Eusebius is relating what *St Luke* says about Paul's first imprisonment and what *report* says about the second imprisonment. As it stands in Euthalius the structure of the sentence is harsh enough : but it all becomes clear when we refer to the History which tells us:

Καὶ Λουκᾶς δὲ ὁ τὰς πράξεις τῶν ἀποστόλων γραφῇ παραδοὺς, ἐν τούτοις κατέλυσε τὴν ἱστορίαν, διετίαν ὅλην ἐπὶ τῆς Ῥώμης τὸν Παῦλον ἄνετον διατρίψαι καὶ τὸν τοῦ Θεοῦ λόγον ἀκωλύτως κηρύξαι ἐπισημηνάμενος. Τότε μὲν οὖν ἀπολογησάμενον αὖθις ἐπὶ τὴν τοῦ κηρύγματος διακονίαν λόγος ἔχει στείλασθαι τὸν ἀπόστολον.

We see then the way in which Euthalius appropriates his author, and we could easily extend our recognition of the matter borrowed from Eusebius by examination of the immediate context. But, for the present, let it suffice to shew that *the Ecclesiastical History of Eusebius is one of the sources of Euthalius.* A second source may be identified by a reference to c. 3 of the Pauline prologue (Z. p. 529) where Euthalius tells us as follows:

Ἀναγκαῖον δὲ ἡγησάμην ἐν βραχεῖ καὶ τὸν χρόνον ἐπισημειώσασθαι τοῦ κηρύγματος Παυλοῦ ἐκ τῶν χρονικῶν κανόνων Εὐσεβίου τοῦ Παμφίλου τὴν ἀνακεφαλαίωσιν ποιούμενος. ἔνθα δὴ τὴν βίβλον μετὰ χεῖρας εἰληφώς κτέ., where from the very language we are led to expect that quotations are coming, or at all events, statements which are the equivalent of quotations. And we shall shew that Euthalius actually had the Chronicon open before him, as well as the History to which, as we have already pointed out, he refers on a subsequent page.

He begins his extracts by saying that the Passion of our Lord occurred in the 18th year of Tiberius. The passage of the Chronicon from which this is taken is preserved in Syncellus (614. 7):

Ἰησοῦς ὁ Χριστὸς ὁ υἱὸς τοῦ θεοῦ ὁ κύριος ἡμῶν κατὰ τὰς περὶ αὐτοῦ προφητείας ἐπὶ τὸ πάθος προῄει ἔτους ιθ' τῆς Τιβερίου βασιλείας.

The Hieronymian version of the Chronicon gives the xviiith year, the Armenian agrees with Syncellus in giving the xixth year.

Euthalius then alludes to the election of the seven deacons, and in particular of Stephen, in the following terms:

καὶ μεθ' ἡμέρας τινὰς ὀλίγας εἶδον ἐκεῖ προχειριζομένους τοὺς Ἀποστόλους εἰς διακονίαν τὸν αὐτοφερώνυμον Στέφανον καὶ τοὺς ἀμφὶ αὐτόν.

Of this we find, in spite of Euthalius' express statement, no trace in the Chronicon, but on looking into the History (*H. E.* ii. 1) we find

καθίστανται...εἰς διακονίαν...ἄνδρες δεδοκιμασμένοι τὸν ἀριθμὸν ἑπτὰ οἱ ἀμφὶ τὸν Στέφανον, where the coincidences in language will be noticed, and then a little lower Eusebius speaks of Stephen as follows:

πρῶτος τὸν αὐτῷ φερώνυμον τῶν ἀξιονίκων τοῦ Χριστοῦ μαρτύρων ἀποφέρεται στέφανον[1].

And here a curious fact comes to light, viz. that Euthalius has failed to understand Eusebius' language.

Eusebius speaks of Stephen as bearing away the martyr's crown, which is appropriately named (στέφανος) for him. Here the play upon words has taken Euthalius' fancy, but he has blunderingly carried off αὐτῷ φερώνυμον and applied it to Stephen, without mentioning the crown to complete the parallel. He might have contented himself with calling Stephen φερώνυμος and leaving his readers to see the obvious play upon the name; but he was appropriating from Eusebius, and not 'mixing his paints with brains,' and so we have the impossible reading which appears in Cod. Boeclerianus as αὐτῷ φερώνυμον, in other MSS. as a single impossible word αὐτοφερώνυμον, in Cod. Lollinianus by emendation as πάνυ φερώνυμον[2].

And lest there should be any doubt about the fact that Euthalius has been appropriating Eusebian language, we can compare with the foregoing passage from Eusebius the language in which Euthalius speaks of the martyrdom of Paul (Z. 522):

τῷ τῶν ἱερονίκων Χριστοῦ μαρτύρων στεφάνῳ κατεκοσμήθη.

Cf. also Euseb. *Mart. Pal.* 3 τὸν τῶν ἱερονίκων τῆς θεοσεβείας ἀθλητῶν στέφανον ἀπηνέγκατο,

and *Mart. Pal.* 9 θείῳ κατεκοσμήθη μαρτυρίῳ etc.

Euthalius continues his discussion of the Pauline chronology, and presently he makes the statement that Paul continued

---

[1] With this compare Syncellus, 621. 4: Ἑπτὰ τὸν ἀριθμὸν, δοκεῖ μοι, πρὸς ὑπηρεσίαν τῶν ἀδελφῶν ὑπὸ τῶν ἀποστόλων κατεστάθησαν· ὧν πρῶτος ἦν Στέφανος ὁ πρῶτος μετὰ τὸν σωτῆρα παρὰ τῶν κυριοκτόνων λιθοβοληθεὶς καὶ τὸν φερώνυμον ἀξίως ὑπενεγκάμενος στέφανον ὑπὲρ αὐτοῦ.

[2] I was wrong in defending this last reading; let the barbarism stand.

preaching from the 19th year of Tiberius to the 13th year of Claudius, ἡγεμονεύοντος τότε τῆς Ἰουδαίας Φήλικος ἐφ' οὗ κατηγορηθεὶς ὑπὸ Ἰουδαίων τὴν ἀπολογίαν ἐποιήσατο Παῦλος.

Turning to the Chronicon we find the following entries from Syncellus:

(629. 3) Κλαύδιος Φήλικα τῆς Ἰουδαίας ἡγεμόνα ἐξεπέμψε.

(632. 17) ἐπὶ αὐτοῦ Παῦλος ὑπὸ Ἰουδαίων κατηγορηθεὶς τὴν ἀπολογίαν πεποίηται.

After describing Paul's appeal to Rome, Euthalius continues (Z. 531):

συνῆν δὲ αὐτῷ καὶ Ἀρίσταρχος ὃν καὶ εἰκότως συναιχμάλωτόν που τῶν ἐπιστολῶν ἀποκαλεῖ, καὶ Λουκᾶς ὁ τὰς πράξεις τῶν Ἀποστόλων γραφῇ παραδούς.

But this is taken, word for word, from the History (*H. E.* ii. 22): and shortly after this the quotation from the History is continued in language which we transcribed above.

A little lower down Euthalius tells us, against which we will set the Eusebian parallels, as follows:

Euthal. (Z. 532).

ἀνεῖλεν μὲν Ἀγριππίναν πρῶτα τὴν ἰδίαν μητέρα, ἔτι δὲ καὶ τὴν ἀδελφὴν τοῦ πατρός, καὶ Ὀκταουΐαν τὴν ἑαυτῷ γυναῖκα καὶ ἄλλους μυρίους τῷ γένει προσήκοντας.

Euthalius continues:

μετέπειτα δὲ καθολικὸν ἐκίνησε διωγμὸν κατὰ τῶν Χριστιανῶν, καὶ οὕτως ἐπὶ τὰς κατὰ τῶν Ἀποστόλων ἐπήρθη σφαγάς.

Euseb. *H. E.* ii. 25.

μητέρα δὲ ὁμοίως καὶ ἀδελφοὺς καὶ γυναῖκα σὺν καὶ ἄλλοις μυρίοις τῷ γένει προσήκουσι....

Euseb. *Chron.* ap. Syncell. 636. 8.

Νέρων ἀνεῖλε τὴν ἑαυτοῦ μητέρα Ἀγριππίναν καὶ τὴν τοῦ πατρὸς ἀδελφήν.

Euseb. *Chron. Armen.*

Neron cum aliis viris illustribus et Hochtabiam uxorem suam interfecit.

Euseb. *Chron.* ap. Cedrenum 360. 17.

καὶ ἄλλους μυρίους τῷ γένει προσήκοντας.

Euseb. *H. E.* ii. 25.

ταύτῃ γοῦν οὗτος θεομάχος ἐν τοῖς μάλιστα πρῶτος ἀνακηρυχθείς, ἐπὶ τὰς κατὰ τῶν Ἀποστόλων ἐπήρθη σφαγάς· and cf. *Chron.* ap. Syncell. 644. 2.

ἐπὶ πᾶσι δ' αὐτοῦ τοῖς ἀτυχήμασι καὶ τὸν πρῶτον κατὰ Χριστιανῶν ἐνεδείξατο διωγμόν...

ἐπὶ πᾶσι δ' αὐτοῦ ἀδικήμασι καὶ τὸν πρῶτον κατὰ Χριστιανῶν ἐνεδείξατο διωγμόν, ἡνίκα Πέτρος καὶ Παῦλος κτέ.

After calculating the years from the Passion to the Martyrdom of Paul (which is evidently reckoned by the aid of the Chronicon), we find that he has turned back to *H. E.* ii. 22 and is working very literally:

Euthalius (Z. 533)

περὶ μὲν τῆς πρώτης αὐτοῦ ἀπολογίας φάσκων 'τάδε· ἐν τῇ πρώτῃ μου ἀπολογίᾳ¹...ἐκ στόματος λέοντος, τοῦτον τὸν Νέρωνα εἶναι λέγων· περὶ δὲ τῆς δευτέρας ἐν ᾗ καὶ τελειοῦται τῷ κατ' αὐτὸν μαρτυρίῳ, φησὶν, τὴν καλήν διακονίαν σου πληροφόρησον. ἐγὼ γὰρ ἤδη σπένδομαι²...ἐφέστηκε. καὶ ὅτι Λουκᾶς ἦν πάλιν σὺν αὐτῷ κτέ,

with which we may compare

Euseb. H. E. ii. 22

ἐν τῇ πρώτῃ μου, φησὶν, ἀπολογίᾳ...λέοντος, τὸν Νέρωνα ταύτῃ, ὡς ἔοικε, διὰ τὸ ὠμόθυμον προσειπὼν...ἐν τῇ αὐτῇ προλέγει γραφῇ φάσκων· ἐγὼ γὰρ ἤδη σπένδομαι...ἐφέστηκεν.

But enough has been said to shew that Euthalius is for the most of his time a plagiarist, as well as sometimes a blunderer. Will it be said in reply that it was quite natural that he should use the Chronicon and the History in writing the life of the Apostle Paul, and that, at all events, he has confessed to borrowing? It usually happens that debts confessed are only a fraction of those contracted, and an examination of the rest of Euthalius' work will confirm that proposition. If he should be original anywhere, it ought to be in his opening remarks, where he explains the scope of the work which he has undertaken and is untrammelled by history or by chronology. But is it so? Let us turn to the prologue to the Acts (Z. p. 404), and see whether it reads like the work of an original and fecund mind. We find him telling us of the new and difficult path that he has to tread in making his edition of the Acts: οἶά τις πῶλος ἀβαδὴς ἢ νέος ἀμαθὴς ἐρήμην ὁδὸν καὶ ἀτριβῆ ἰέναι προστεταγμένος. οὐδένα γάρ που τῶν ὅσοι τὸν θεῖον ἐπρεσβεύσαντο λόγον εἰς δεῦρο διέγνων περὶ τοῦτο τῆς γραφῆς ταύτης εἰς σπουδὴν πεποιη-μένον τὸ σχῆμα.

¹ 2 Tim. iv. 16.   ² 2 Tim. iv. 5.

But when we turn to the opening chapter of the Ecclesiastical History, the secret is out, for here we find

ἐπεὶ καὶ πρῶτοι νῦν τῆς ὑποθέσεως ἐπιβάντες οἰά τινα ἐρήμην καὶ ἀτριβῆ ἰέναι ὁδὸν ἐγχειροῦμεν,

and somewhat further on

Ἀναγκαιότατα δέ μοι πονεῖσθαι τὴν ὑπόθεσιν ἡγοῦμαι ὅτι μηδένα πω εἰς δεῦρο τῶν ἐκκλησιαστικῶν συγγραφέων διέγνων περὶ τοῦτο τῆς γραφῆς σπουδὴν πεποιημένον τὸ μέρος.

Further the expression ὅσοι τὸν θεῖον ἐπρεσβεύσαντο λόγον may be compared with the opening sentences of Eusebius ὅσοι τε κατὰ γενεὰν ἑκάστην ἀγράφως ἢ καὶ διὰ συγγραμμάτων τὸν θεῖον ἐπρέσβευσαν λόγον κτέ.

Other coincidences in thought and expression may be noted [1], and it follows that the loans which Euthalius makes on Eusebius are not limited to a single section, but that he is a systematic plagiarist.

It will be admitted, I think, that the dependence of Euthalius upon Eusebius is established: but it may well be questioned whether it does not go much further than our identifications, and whether it does not involve other authors beside Eusebius.

Take, for example, the Pauline prologue in which Euthalius speaks in such choice language of the reasons which led him to his task, and of his own ecclesiastical obedience to the superiors who set him at the work. At first sight these sentences appear to be the most original in the whole document and to have the flavour of real history. No one would suspect, at the first reading of these personal statements on the part of Euthalius, that they constitute a conventional opening peto to a new book. But that such is the case will, I think, be clear by comparing with the language of Euthalius the opening sentences of the Armenian historian, Lazarus of Pharbi.

---

[1] e.g. (Z. 405) συγγνώμην γε πλείστην αἰτῶν ἐπ' ἀμφοῖν, τόλμης ὁμοῦ καὶ προπετείας τῆς ἐμῆς.

Euseb. H. E. i. 1 ἀλλὰ μοι συγγνώμην ἤδη εὐγνωμόνων ἐντεῦθεν ὁ λόγος αἰτεῖ, with which cf. H. E. vi. 20 τὴν περὶ τὸ συντάττειν καινὰς γραφὰς προπέτειάν τε καὶ τόλμαν ἐπιστομίζων.

The pilfering runs through the prologue to the Acts. Cf. (Z. 410) Ἀντιοχεὺς γὰρ οὗτος ὑπάρχων τὸ γένος, ἰατρός τε τὴν ἐπιστήμην, πρὸς Παύλου μαθητευθείς, with Euseb. H. E. iii. 4 Λουκᾶς δὲ τὸ μὲν γένος ὢν τῶν ἀπ' Ἀντιοχείας, τὴν δὲ ἐπιστήμην ἰατρός, τὰ πλεῖστα συγγεγονὼς τῷ Παύλῳ....

Euthalius.

Prol. in Epp. Paul.

Τὸ φιλομαθὲς καὶ σπουδαῖον ἀγάμενος τῆς σῆς ἀγάπης, Πάτερ τιμιώτατε, αἰδοῖ τε καὶ πειθοῖ εἴκων, στενωπῷ τινι καὶ παρεισδύσει τῆς ἱστορίας ἐμαυτὸν ἐπαφῆκα, τονδὲ τὸν πρόλογον τοῦ Παύλου πραγματείας συγγράψαι· καὶ πολὺ μεῖζον ἢ καθ' ἡμᾶς ἔργον ἀνεδεξάμην δέει τῆς παρακοῆς· ἔγνων γὰρ ἐν παροιμίαις τὸ λαλούμενον, ὅτι δὴ υἱὸς ἀνήκοος ἐν ἀπωλείᾳ ἔσται, ὁ δὲ ὑπήκοος ἔσται ταύτης ἐκτός (cf. Prov. 13. 1).

Lazarus of Pharbi.

History of Armenia.

Written at the request of Vahan, general and marzban of Armenia.

(Translation of Victor Langlois.)

Le présent ouvrage, œuvre de notre faiblesse, va ·former comme la troisième partie de ces annales. Nous sommes forcé d' [entreprendre] un semblable travail par ordre des princes et sur les exhortations des saints docteurs, n'osant pas nous opposer, en nous rappelant les menaces que la saint Écriture fait aux enfants désobéissants et de l'indulgence [qu'elle] montre vis-à-vis de ceux qui sont soumis et dociles.

Here the same idea is seen to underlie both authors, viz. the fear of disobedience to superiors, based on the warning of the Scriptures against disobedient children. The passage which Euthalius quotes from the Proverbs underlies the prologue of Lazarus. Each writer suggests by antithesis, in the manner of the Proverbs, the well-being which is the portion of the obedient. Each of them speaks modestly of his own powers, Lazarus calling the task one that is 'the work of his weakness,' and Euthalius 'a work that is too great for me.'

Euthalius further describes his work by saying that he has rushed into 'the narrows and straits of history' in writing the present prologue to St Paul.

Surely the natural suggestion is that both writers are using conventional openings, and Euthalius' language suggests further that he has borrowed from the prologue *to a history*.

Lazarus wrote his History not earlier than A.D. 485 as a sequel to the works of Agathangelus and Faustus of Byzantium. Euthalius cannot have imitated him, both by reason of the date, as well as because the work is written in Armenian. Will it be said that Lazarus has imitated the Euthalian prologue? this is extremely unlikely, for Lazarus was well acquainted with Greek literature and was hardly likely to select for a model of style so trifling a piece as Euthalius' prologue. Moreover when we take into account the proved borrowing of Euthalius from Eusebius and the

suspicious statement about the 'narrows and straits of history'
we are led to infer that both writers are drawing upon some
classic opening in which the work of a historical writer is compared
to the course of a ship navigated in difficult and narrow seas.
And this supposition is not an unnatural one. It will be
found to be the main idea of the prologue to the history of Agathangelus, who tells us (Langlois, p. 106) " Pour nous, ce n'est pas
une orgueilleuse résolution qui nous pousse à entreprendre temé-
rairement ce travail; mais nous sommes contraint malgré nous,
par les ordres formels des princes, à naviguer sur la mer des
lettres." And a reference of the prologue of Euthalius to the
Catholic Epistles shews the same comparison of the literary artist
to the tempest-tossed voyager in a tiny skiff.

We say, then, that the evidence favours a belief that Euthalius
found a literary model for his prologue to the Pauline Epistles in
the proem of some well-known historical work; and from the
suspicious use of a quotation from the Proverbs we suspect that
it was the work of a Christian historian. And certainly we do
not think any one will have anything further to say in defence of
the originality of Euthalius or in praise of his copious vocabulary.

Having now proved the dependence of Euthalius upon Eusebius and others we are in a better position to determine the text
of Euthalius in doubtful cases and the interpretation where the
meaning is obscure.

For example, in a passage quoted above (Z. 532) the printed
text of Euthalius reads ἀνεῖλεν μὲν 'Αγριππίναν πρῶτα τὴν ἰδίαν
μητέρα where Cod. Vat. 761 has τὴν ἑαυτοῦ μητέρα. A reference
to the Eusebian text shews that this latter reading is probably
correct.

On the same page Euthalius has συνῆλθε δὲ πάλιν ὁ Λουκᾶς
αὐτῷ, but Cod. Vat. 761 and Cod. Boeclerianus read συνῆν. A
reference to the text of Eusebius shews that he constantly, and in
this very connection reads συνῆν. Conversely, where the text of
Eusebius is doubtful, we have reason to believe that the Euthalian
extracts furnish fresh material for its elucidation.

Coming now to the question of interpretation, we have a right
to assume as a general principle that when Euthalius uses
Eusebian language he uses it in the Eusebian sense; he may
sometimes misunderstand, but even a stupid transcriber will, in
the majority of cases, take the words in their proper sense. Let

us then turn to the disputed passage in which I claim to have detected a deletion of the unorthodox name Meletius and the insertion of the orthodox Athanasius, and in which Mr Robinson thinks no case has been made out for any tampering with the text.

The principal sentences which need interpretation are as follows:

(Z. 406) ἐγὼ δὲ δικαιώτατα, καὶ μάλα γε ὀρθῶς, σύντροφόν τε καὶ φιλὴν ἐπιφημίσαιμ᾽ ἄν σοι, καὶ καταλέξω τὴν εὐπροσήγορον, τὴν πάνυ φερώνυμον, τὴν τῶν θείων λογίων ἐμφιλόσοφόν φημι μελέτην, ὑφ᾽ ἣν γεγωνὼς, φιλόχριστε, καὶ εἴσωγέ τοι τῶν δικτύων αὐτῆς ὑπάρχων, καὶ τὴν ἐράσμιον αὐτῆς προσηγορίαν ἐγκαταπραγματευόμενος συχναῖς τε ἀεὶ καὶ ἀκοιμήτοις γυμνασίαις ἀκουόμενος (l. ἀσκούμενος) εὐθαλεστάτην κατέστησας.

Starting from the known fact that Euthalius is a careful student of Eusebius, we naturally ask the question whether Eusebius uses the word φερώνυμος, which is a little difficult of interpretation, and what meaning he attaches to it.

We have already given one instance in which Euthalius plays on the name of Stephen, and the crown, φερώνυμος αὐτῷ, that is involved in that name, and have shewn that the word-play was based upon a similar one in the text of Eusebius, which Euthalius has blunderingly appropriated.

But it is when we come to look into the text of Eusebius generally that we find the meaning of the disputed word and discover that it is one of the commonest literary artifices of Eusebius to indulge in an etymological subtlety over the names of the people whom he describes. Let us take some cases.

H. E. iv. 16. Eusebius describes the philosophy of Crescens the opponent of Justin by saying τὸν φερώνυμον δὲ οὗτος τῇ Κυνικῇ προσηγορίᾳ βίου τε καὶ τρόπον ἐζήλου.

The mode of life of Crescens was appropriately named after the Cynic or Canine philosophy.

H. E. v. 24 (which, I see, Prof. Robinson also refers to) Καὶ ὁ μὲν Εἰρηναῖος, φερώνυμός τις ὢν τῇ προσηγορίᾳ, αὐτῷ τε τῷ τρόπῳ εἰρηνοποιός, τοιαῦτα ὑπὲρ τῆς τῶν ἐκκλησιῶν εἰρήνης παρεκάλει, where the meaning is sufficiently clear.

H. E. vii.. 32 describing the bishop Theodotos, Eusebius speaks of him as πράγμασιν αὐτοῖς ἀνὴρ καὶ τὸ κύριον ὄνομα καὶ τὸν ἐπίσκοπον ἐπαληθεύσας, a man who verified by his actions his proper name (i.e. as involved in the interpretation of Theodotos, or God-bestowed) and the name of bishop.

H. E. ix. 2. In the same way Theotecnos, the persecutor, is spoken of as δεινὸς καὶ γόης καὶ πονηρὸς ἀνὴρ καὶ τῆς προσωνυμίας ἀλλότριος. No child of God he! Somewhat more obscure is the passage *Mart. Pal.* 8, in which Eusebius speaks of the martyrs in the Porphyritic mine in the Thebaid: εἶχε μὲν πρὸ τούτου τὸ καλούμενον ἐν Θηβαΐδι φερωνύμως οὗ γεννᾶται Πορφυρίτου λίθου μέταλλον πλείστην ὅσην πληθὺν τῶν τῆς θεοσεβείας ὁμολογητῶν: a sentence which the contemporary Syriac version interprets as follows: "great multitudes of confessors were in the mines that are called Porphyrites, in the country of Thebais, which is on one side of Egypt: and on account of the purple marble which is in that land the name of Porphyrites has also been given to those who were employed in cutting it."

There is no doubt Eusebius is playing upon the name Πορφυρίτης, but whether we have the Greek sentence in its original form is a little doubtful.

A still more difficult case to interpret is *Mart. Pal.* 9, where a persecutor is spoken of, Μάξυς ὄνομα, χείρων τῆς προσηγορίας ἄνθρωπος. The word Μάξυς does not seem to be Greek, and an attempt has been made, not very successfully, to give it a Syriac etymology (see Ruinart, *Act. Sinc.* p. 287).

The word φερωνύμως is used also with reference to the name of a disease, which, for the present investigation, is much the same as a proper name, and Eusebius says, in describing a pestilence that had broken out, *H. E.* ix. 8 ἕλκος δὲ ἦν φερωνύμως τοῦ πυρώδους ἕνεκεν ἄνθραξ προσαγορευόμενον, 'there was a sore that was rightly called *carbuncle* on account of its inflammatory nature.'

Very similar is the way in which Eusebius plays upon the name of the heretic Manes, whom he describes, *H. E.* vii. 31, as ὁ μανεὶς τὰς φρένας, ἐπώνυμός τε τῆς δαιμονώσης αἱρέσεως...δαιμονικός τις ὢν καὶ μανιώδης...τυφούμενος ἐπὶ τῇ μανίᾳ[1].

But perhaps most striking of all is the way in which he plays with the name of *Meletius* the bishop of the churches in Pontus (*H. E.* vii. 32): ὁ δὲ Μελέτιος (τὸ μέλι τῆς Ἀττικῆς ἐκάλουν αὐτὸν

---

[1] Similarly Titus Bostrensis adv. *Manichaeos*, Prol.: ὁ δὲ Μαντῆς ἐκ βαρβάρων καὶ τῆς μανίας αὐτῆς ἐπώνυμος.

οἱ ἀπὸ παιδείας) τοιοῦτος ἦν οἷον ἂν γράψειέ τις τῶν κατὰ πάντα
λόγων ἕνεκα τελεώτατον.

There can be no reason to doubt, then, from the cases of word-
play which we find applied in Eusebius to proper names, that
Euthalius has been imitating a literary peculiarity of the
Ecclesiastical History: and in the case of the play upon the
name of Stephen, he was found guilty of the theft, *flagrante
delicto.*

And it follows from this that when we read his description of
the attractive Melete who ensnares holy fathers in her net, and
calls her φερώνυμος, we are to expect a pun.   Moreover when in
Eusebius we find that he uses in connection with his φερωνύμως,
the expression φερώνυμος τῇ προσηγορίᾳ, we can scarcely doubt
that when Euthalius describes Miss Melete as τὴν εὐπροσήγορον,
τὴν πάνυ φερώνυμον, he means, not that she is *affable,* or *easy of
access,* but that she is *rightly named :* so that the repetition of two
almost equivalent expressions accentuates the belief that there is
some play upon the word[1].   The only thing left to determine is
what the word-play consists in.   According to Prof. Robinson it
is nothing more than a play upon the alternative meanings of
Study and Training : in support of which it might be pointed out
that Eusebius, whose cast-off garments furnish Euthalius' ward-
robe, uses the word in both senses.   So much might be readily
admitted.

But to this explanation there are objections from every
quarter: Eusebius in the cases which we have quoted plays
almost exclusively upon titles and proper names, such as Cynic,
Irenaeus, Theodotos, Theotecnos, Porphyrite, Maxys, Manes, and
Meletius.   The only exception, and that is more apparent than
real, is when he describes the disease called Anthrax and says it
was rightly named.

Euthalius also in three cases (Stephen, Saul, and Paul) expounds
proper names; and the presumption, therefore, is that something
of the same kind is involved in the description of Melete as
φερώνυμος and εὐπροσήγορος.   The conditions are perfectly
satisfied by the assumption that the person addressed is named
Meletius.   Euthalius might, to be sure, have called Meletius
φερώνυμος and left us to imagine what he meant, but it answered

---

[1] With which previous explanation of mine, I see Mr Robinson agrees.

his purpose just as well to call Melete φερώνυμος, the father
Meletius having been already mentioned in the context.
On Prof. Robinson's supposition, we have a play upon words
which is (i) obscure, and (ii) not of sufficient importance in view
of the space which is occupied by the praises of Melete. From
the very beginning of the prologue to the Acts the play upon the
word betrays itself, and the allusions to Study are kept up almost
to the end of the prologue. It is evidently the nucleus of the
composition. Is it possible that one doubtful oscillation between
the senses of Study and Training could have exercised such an
influence upon the mind of Euthalius as to colour the whole of the
dedication of his work?

But this is not all: we are able to shew that the name of
Meletius was a name that was commonly played with. When I
first announced that I believed there were traces of the erasure of
this name in the Euthalian prologue, it never occurred to me
that a parallel instance could be found of the literary trick which
I had, as I supposed, unearthed. I simply saw that Euthalius
made puns (often bad ones[1]), and suggested that he had made one
more than the three of which he was proved to be guilty. But I
discovered subsequently, and added a note to that effect, that
Gregory of Nazianzus had called Meletius of Antioch his 'honey-
sweet' friend, in the following lines:

> Carm. xi. 1521 τὸν ὄνθ᾽ ὅπερ κέκλητο καὶ καλούμενον
> ὃ ἦν· Μέλιτος γὰρ τρόπος καὶ τοὔνομα.

If Gregory of Nazianzus played with the name of his
Meletius, there was certainly nothing against the supposition that
Euthalius might have treated one of his friends in a similar
manner.

But surely the case is immensely strengthened when we find
amongst the names upon which Eusebius plays *the very name of
Meletius*; for we have shewn conclusively that Euthalius appropriates the ideas and language of Eusebius freely, and that he
imitates him in playing upon the name of Stephen. Why then
should there be any difficulty in the supposition that Euthalius
has also borrowed from Eusebius the idea of playing upon the
name of Meletius? And is not this hypothesis further strengthened

---

[1] I refuse to credit Eusebius with Σαῦλος ὅτι ἐσάλευεν or with Παῦλος ὅτι
πέπαυται.

by the fact that in the very same sentence, as Mr Robinson admits, Euthalius plays upon his own name? I consider, then, that my case, so far from having been rendered hopeless, or reduced to an unnecessary piece of ingenuity in the face of Prof. Robinson's investigations, is in reality very much stronger than I had at first imagined it to be[1].

A further test of the accuracy of the solution will lie in the fact that it helps us to clear up some of the remaining obscurities in the text of Euthalius.

For instance in the opening sentences of the prologue to the Acts, we are told of students of the Scripture in quest of immortality, who seek to realize the blessing of the first Psalm,

τοὺς περὶ τοῦ θείου λόγου λόγους ἐμμελέτημα νύκτωρ τε καὶ μεθ᾽ ἡμέραν, τῇ σφῶν αὐτῶν τέθεινται ψυχῇ, ἀληθῶς τὸ τῆς ἀγλαοφεγγοῦς καὶ μακαρίας ταύτης [τροφῆς] ἡμεροτρωθέντες, καὶ τῶν ἐναρέτων αὐτῆς καὶ θείων καρπῶν ἀπογευσάμενοι.

The passage is difficult to understand, and Zacagni, apparently in despair, has inserted *de suo* the word τροφῆς and translates as if people were 'daily fed upon this blessed meat'! But this will not do: ἡμεροτρωθέντες cannot mean 'supplied from day to day'; if it means anything it means 'gently pierced'; but as a matter of fact, there is no such word. And certainly if τροφῆς were rightly restored, the author could not go on to speak of 'tasting her divine fruits,' i.e. the fruits of the τροφή. But suppose we leave out the word added by Zacagni and read the clause

τῷ τῆς ἀγλαοφεγγοῦς καὶ μακαρίας ταύτης ἱμέρῳ τρωθέντες

'smitten with passion for this resplendent and blessed creature,' we see that all that is necessary to the sense is a satisfactory feminine antecedent to the clause. And this is at once supplied by writing μελέτην for ἐμμελέτημα, which thinly disguises it. The personification of μελέτη is the key to the perplexity of the passage.

We will now pass on to the more difficult question of the genuineness of the *Martyrium Pauli* which is usually attached to the Euthalian prologue to the Pauline Epistles. As we have pointed out, this question is not really much affected by the

---

[1] The only alternative would be to credit some lost book of Eusebius with the playful preface addressed to Meletius, who would in that case be Meletius of Pontus, who was seven years in hiding in Palestine during the persecution recorded by Eusebius and in constant intercourse with that father. But we do not need to resort to this hypothesis.

solution of the previous one. We might find a Meletius to whom Euthalius could dedicate his work almost anywhere in the fourth century. So that it is not necessary to decide the Meletian question before discussing the *Martyrium*. It must, however, be remembered that the dependence of Euthalius upon Eusebius is a factor in the solution of both questions, and this dependence is a proved and demonstrated fact.

Let us see whether it has any bearing upon the discussion by which Prof. Robinson seeks to shew the dependence of the *Martyrium* upon the Pauline prologue, and its non-authenticity as a work of Euthalius.

On p. 29 of his *Euthaliana* Mr Robinson prints for the purposes of comparison the passages of the prologue which correspond to the *Martyrium*; as follows :

Prologue to Pauline Epistles.

Z. 522. Αὐτόθι οὖν ὁ μακάριος Παῦλος τὸν καλὸν ἀγῶνα ἀγωνισάμενος, ὥς φησιν αὐτός, τῷ τῶν ἱερονίκων Χριστοῦ μαρτύρων στεφάνῳ κατεκοσμήθη. Ῥωμαῖοι δὲ περικαλλέσιν οἴκοις καὶ βασιλείοις τούτου λείψανα καθείρξαντες ἐπέτειον αὐτῷ μνήμης ἡμέραν πανηγυρίζουσι τῇ πρὸ τριῶν καλανδῶν Ἰουλίων πέμπτῃ Πανέμου μηνὸς τούτου τὸ μαρτύριον ἑορτάζοντες.

Z. 532. Ἔνθα δὴ συνέβη τὸν Παῦλον τριακοστῷ ἕκτῳ ἔτει τοῦ σωτηρίου πάθους τρισκαιδεκάτῳ δὲ Νέρωνος μαρτυρῆσαι, ξίφει τὴν κεφαλὴν ἀποτμηθέντα.

Z. 533. Περὶ δὲ τῆς δευτέρας (ἀπολογίας) ἐν ᾗ καὶ τελειοῦται τῷ κατ' αὐτὸν μαρτυρίῳ, φησὶν κτέ. Ἔστιν οὖν ὁ πᾶς χρόνος τοῦ κηρύγματος Παύλου κτέ.

Z. 529. Ἀναγκαῖον δὲ ἡγησάμην ἐν βραχεῖ καὶ τὸν χρόνον ἐπισημειώσασθαι τοῦ κηρύγματος Παύλου, ἐκ τῶν χρονικῶν κανόνων Εὐσεβίου τοῦ Παμφίλου τὴν ἀνακεφαλαίωσιν ποιούμενος.

Μαρτύριον Παύλου τοῦ Ἀποστόλου. Ἐπὶ Νέρωνος τοῦ Καίσαρος Ῥωμαίων ἐμαρτύρησεν αὐτόθι Παῦλος ὁ ἀπόστολος, ξίφει τὴν κεφαλὴν ἀποτμηθείς, ἐν τῷ τριακοστῷ καὶ ἕκτῳ ἔτει τοῦ σωτηρίου πάθους, τὸν καλὸν ἀγῶνα ἀγωνισάμενος ἐν Ῥώμη, πέμπτῃ ἡμέρᾳ Πανέμου μηνὸς ἥτις λέγοιτο ἂν παρὰ Ῥωμαίοις ἡ πρὸ τριῶν καλανδῶν Ἰουλίων, καθ' ἣν ἐτελειώθη ὁ ἅγιος ἀπόστολος τῷ κατ' αὐτὸν μαρτυρίῳ ἑξηκοστῷ καὶ ἐννάτῳ ἔτει τῆς τοῦ σωτῆρος ἡμῶν Ἰησοῦ τοῦ παρουσίας. Ἔστιν οὖν ὁ πᾶς χρόνος ἐξ οὗ ἐμαρτύρησε τριακόσια τριάκοντα ἔτη μέχρι τῆς παρούσης ταύτης ὑπατείας, τετάρτης μὲν Ἀρκαδίου τρίτης δὲ Ὀνωρίου τῶν δύο ἀδελφῶν αὐτοκρατόρων Αὐγούστων, ἐννάτης ἰνδικτιῶνος τῆς πεντεκαιδεκαετηρικῆς περιόδου, μηνὸς Ἰουνίου εἰκοστῇ ἐννάτη ἡμέρᾳ. Ἐσημειωσάμην ἀκριβῶς τὸν χρόνον τοῦ μαρτυρίου Παύλου ἀποστόλου.

We have printed this passage with the spaced type by which

Prof. Robinson indicates the coincidence between the two sets of statements. His first remark upon these coincidences is that the comparison 'disposes of Zacagni's view that it is the work of the early Father from whom Euthalius borrowed his chapter-divisions, for it is redolent of Euthalius: the only question is whether it is not too redolent.' It will be recognized at once that this question of redolence has been somewhat complicated by the proved dependence of Euthalius upon Eusebius. The prologue itself has 'an ancient and fish-like smell.' Almost every word of it is from Eusebius, as we will shew in detail. And consequently when Mr Robinson makes his first general criticism of the *Martyrium* by saying that 'it is almost inconceivable that a writer who has so great a wealth of expression as the author of the Prologue should repeat his own language in this slavish manner,' we may very well reply that the objection disappears as soon as it is found that the wealth of language is an illusion, and that the repetition is a repetition of the words of some other person. There is no law of criticism which expresses in the language of minute probability the chance that a person who has made a patchwork out of some other person's writings will repeat the offence or which affirms the extreme unlikeliness that he will put the stolen pieces together a little differently. We come now to three detailed objections which Mr Robinson makes to the authenticity of the *Martyrium*, which would be fatal if they were all correctly taken, without the possibility of reply: we will take them in order: they are intended to demonstrate that the *Martyrium* is a later document, produced by an epitomiser working on the former.

1. At first the author of the *Martyrium* embodies from the Prologue the Roman date for June 29, viz. ἡ πρὸ τριῶν καλανδῶν Ἰουλίων; but later on he gives the date as μηνὸς Ἰουνίου εἰκοστῇ ἐννάτῃ ἡμέρᾳ.

2. It is objected that the phrase in the *Martyrium* τῷ κατ' αὐτὸν μαρτυρίῳ is extremely harsh, whether αὐτὸν be referred to Paul or Nero; but in the Prologue it is quite clear that it is referred to Nero. The obscurity in the *Martyrium* is due to the careless work of the epitomiser.

3. The strongest objection of all lies in the fact that the *Martyrium* places the actual martyrdom on June 29th, which is a deduction from the fact that the Roman Church kept the

festival of SS. Peter and Paul on that day, which we know from the Liberian catalogue (A.D. 354) to have been simply the day of the Deposition in A.D. 258. This mistake, according to Mr Robinson, was not made by the author of the Prologue. These are formidable objections; it only remains to see whether they can claim to be insuperable.

Probably the best way to proceed will be to try and get a clear idea of how much of the matter quoted from the Prologue is Euthalius and how much Eusebius.

To begin with, the adverb αὐτόθι, which stands at the head of the first extract, is a Eusebian word, probably the most frequent adverb which he employs, and quite one of his style-words, as any one may see by turning the pages of the History. In Eusebius it never stands, as far as I know, at the beginning of the sentence, and never is far removed from the preceding note of place. Euthalius is struck with it and gives it a prominent position, but at the same time it is thirteen lines of the text since Euthalius has mentioned Rome[1]. Probably in the passage of Eusebius upon which Euthalius was working the matter was better arranged.

The words that follow τῷ τῶν ἱερονίκων Χριστοῦ μαρτύρων στεφάνῳ κατεκοσμήθη we have already shewn to be Eusebian.

We are next told of the Depositio Martyrum, and the curious words are used περικαλλέσιν οἴκοις καὶ βασιλείοις.

Is it Euthalius or Eusebius that speaks of the churches in which the martyrs' bones are laid as 'gorgeous and palatial dwellings'? Let us turn to the oration of Eusebius at the consecration of the Church at Tyre: we find (H. E. x. 4) that he speaks of Christ as having filled the world with his royal dwellings (βασιλικῶν οἴκων αὐτοῦ) which are adorned with περικαλλῆ κοσμήματά τε καὶ ἀναθήματα. Later on in the same discourse he twice speaks of the Church at Tyre in the same style, calling it τὸν βασίλειον οἶκον (pp. 473, 478) and a little later on again it is τὸν μέγαν καὶ βασιλικὸν ἐξ ἁπάντων οἶκον by which he describes the Spiritual Church. We may be pretty sure that Euthalius is working over some Eusebian statement.

The expression τοῦ σωτηρίου πάθους is easily seen to be from

---

[1] The Eusebian usage may be seen from scores of passages; there are three in the beginning of H. E. iii. 5 πρὸς τῶν αὐτόθι στρατοπέδων ἀναγορευθεὶς...τοῦ τὸν αὐτόθι τῆς ἐπισκοπῆς θρόνον...τοὺς αὐτόθι δοκίμοις δι' ἀποκαλύψεως ἐκδοθέντα. The commonest use of the word is in such phrases as ἡ αὐτόθι ἐκκλησία, ἡ αὐτόθι παροικία.

the same source; it is Eusebius' regular term, and occurs not only prominently in the Chronicon, but throughout the History: e.g. *Mart. Pal.* Prol. τῆς τοῦ σωτηρίου πάθους ἑορτῆς, *Mart. Pal.* 11 ταυτὸ τοῦ σωτηρίου μαρτύριον πάθους. Cf. also *H. E.* viii. 2, x. 3. We should not, of course, dwell on comparatively colourless expressions like these, if we had not proved that Eusebius was the principal source for Euthalian language, a fact which entitles us to make identifications of common words and turns of speech as well as rare ones.

The expression τρισκαιδεκάτῳ δὲ Νέρωνος...ἀποτμηθέντα is based partly upon the Chronicon, where the years of Nero are counted separately, but can also be illustrated from *H. E.* ii. 25 ἐπὶ τὰς κατὰ τῶν ἀποστόλων ἐπήρθη σφαγάς· Παῦλος δὴ οὖν ἐπ' αὐτῆς Ῥώμης τὴν κεφαλὴν ἀποτμηθῆναι κτέ., where the only thing we miss is the ξίφει which occurs both in the Prologue and in the *Martyrium*. We have already shewn that Euthalius had pilfered from this passage.

Coming now to the disputed passage ἐν ᾗ καὶ τελειοῦται τῷ κατ' αὐτὸν μαρτυρίῳ we find that this is not Euthalius but Eusebius (*H. E.* ii. 22), δεύτερον δ' ἐπιβάντα τῇ αὐτῇ πόλει, τῷ κατ' αὐτὸν τελειωθῆναι μαρτυρίῳ. And the obscurity which attaches to the phrase κατ' αὐτὸν will be found to be involved in Eusebius himself, so that the *Martyrium* is actually nearer to Eusebius than is the Prologue.

As there seems to be no doubt that Euthalius has transcribed a number of sentences from this chapter of the History it will be convenient to set down the very words of Eusebius, indicating what Euthalius has borrowed in spaced type:

τούτου δὲ Φῆστος ὑπὸ Νέρωνος διάδοχος πέμπεται· καθ' ὃν δικαιολογησάμενος ὁ Παῦλος, δέσμιος ἐπὶ Ῥώμης ἄγεται. Ἀρίσταρχος δ' αὐτῷ συνῆν, ὃν καὶ εἰκότως συναιχμάλωτόν που τῶν ἐπιστολῶν ἀποκαλεῖ. καὶ Λουκᾶς δὲ ὁ τὰς πράξεις τῶν ἀποστόλων γραφῇ παραδούς, ἐν τούτοις κατέλυσε τὴν ἱστορίαν, διετίαν ὅλην ἐπὶ τῆς Ῥώμης τὸν Παῦλον ἄνετον διατρίψαι καὶ τὸν τοῦ Θεοῦ λόγον ἀκωλύτως κηρύξαι ἐπισημηνάμενος. τότε μὲν οὖν [Euthal. add. ἐπὶ Νέρωνος] ἀπολογησάμενον [Euthal. add. τὸν Παῦλον] αὖθις ἐπὶ τὴν τοῦ κηρύγματος διακονίαν λόγος ἔχει στείλασθαι τὸν ἀπόστολον, δεύτερον δ' ἐπιβάντα τῇ αὐτῇ πόλει, τῷ κατ' αὐτὸν τελειωθῆναι μαρτυρίῳ.

I suppose we must explain κατ' αὐτὸν here by reference to καθ' ὃν at the beginning of the chapter[1], but the harshness of the construction is as great in Eusebius as in the *Martyrium*, and no argument for a later date of the *Martyrium* can be deduced from the expression in question. Mr Robinson's second objection, therefore, falls to the ground.

The strongest objection is, no doubt, the third, which is based upon an apparent confusion between the Martyrdom and the Depositio of the Apostles which, according to Robinson, exists in the *Martyrium* but not in the Prologue. Did Eusebius say anything about the Depositio, and did he say it clearly? We have by this time little reason to confide in Euthalius as an independent investigator : and the prejudice is in favour of the use of Eusebian matter. It is very unfortunate that just at this point we lack the reference which would decisively clear the matter up, for Eusebius' book of Martyrs to which he several times refers in his history is not extant. No doubt it contained the Martyrdom of the great Apostles as well as of later worthies. We may, however, get some light upon the matter by referring to *H. E.* iii. 31, where Eusebius records the death of John and Philip and says Παύλου μὲν οὖν καὶ Πέτρου τῆς τελευτῆς ὅ τε χρόνος καὶ ὁ τρόπος καὶ προσέτι ὁ τῆς μετὰ τὴν ἀπαλλαγὴν τοῦ βίου τῶν σκηνωμάτων αὐτῶν καταθέσεως χῶρος, ἤδη πρότερον ἡμῖν δεδήλωται. Here κατάθεσις is the equivalent of the Latin *depositio*, and while at first sight it seems that Eusebius is speaking of the later Depositio and carefully distinguishing it from the Martyrdom, the previous passage in the History to which he refers (*H. E.* ii. 25) shews conclusively that this is not his meaning: he is describing the Depositio of SS. Peter and Paul in the Vatican and in the Church on the Ostian Way. Now this very chapter is one of those from which we have already convicted Euthalius of borrowing ; and we say therefore that not only is the language of the Prologue at the point in question Eusebian language ; but that it certainly does not refer to the Catacombs, for the resting places of the Martyrs are splendid churches, in the plural; this must mean the Vatican and the church on the Ostian Way. It appears therefore that the confusion between the Martyrdom and the Depositio exists equally

---

[1] It is Eusebius' way of describing coincidence in chronological position : *vide* Chronicon *passim*.

in the Prologue and the *Martyrium*. This would seem to meet Mr Robinson's third objection. And now as to the method of dating the Martyrdom or Depositio. In the first place, while we have reason to regard Eusebius as the proximate source for both the Prologue and the *Martyrium*, the actual date given, the 5th of Panemus, is older than Eusebius. We can see this by comparing Eusebius' method of dating Martyrdoms in the account of the Palestine Martyrs. For example, we have Ξανθικὸς μὴν ὃς λέγοιτ᾽ ἂν Ἀπρίλλιος παρὰ Ῥωμαίοις· Δεσίου μηνὸς ἑβδόμῃ, πρὸ ἑπτὰ εἰδῶν Ἰουνίων λέγοιτ᾽ ἂν παρὰ Ῥωμαίοις [1] and so on, from which it is clear that the months used by Eusebius, writing at Cesarea, are the Roman months with Syro-Macedonian names; the Syro-Macedonian calendar has, therefore, been displaced. It is not unreasonable to suppose, then, that a reference to Panemus in the account of Paul's Martyrdom, where Panemus is clearly the Syro-Macedonian month and not the later Roman substitute, belongs to an earlier time than Eusebius. If he found it in his sources, he was almost bound to explain it. The document from which our information comes must have contained more than the allusion to the fifth day of Panemus. But even with the attached Roman date there is still some ambiguity; for Panemus itself has become ambiguous: and we may regard it as certain that the calendar which in Eusebius' time had been changed from Syro-Macedonian arrangement to Roman arrangement, while retaining the names, would in the end take up the Roman names as well as the Roman arrangement of the months : and these names amongst a Greek-speaking people will appear as Greek names. It is therefore quite natural that we should find in the *Martyrium* in the passage in which the writer brings the dates down to his day, the statement that the Martyrdom is commemorated on the 25th of June.

I do not see, then, that any convincing reason has been brought forward for making the *Martyrium* later than the Pauline Prologue, or assigning them to different hands. Euthalius is proved to have been an epitomizer of previous materials; why should we assume a second epitomizer to go over what Euthalius has collected; he was quite capable of doing the summarizing himself, either by

---

[1] That is the 7th of Desius is the 7th of June, and so constantly. Notice the agreement of the Eusebian method of dating with the language of the *Martyrium*: ἥτις λέγοιτ᾽ ἂν παρὰ Ῥωμαίοις.

going over his prologue and picking up the allusions, as Prof. Robinson thinks was done, or by going once more, which is the likelier hypothesis, to the sources from which he had derived his information.

The probability that Euthalius went to his sources for the summary which we find in the *Martyrium* is increased by the appearance in the reckoning of the Eusebian phrase ἥτις λέγοιτ᾽ ἂν in connection with the equivalent date.

There are other reasons for refusing to Euthalius the extreme antiquity with which Mr Robinson wishes to credit him. One of them has been pointed out by Zahn in *Theol. Lit. Blatt* for Dec. 20, 1895; he shews that in Euthalius' list of quotations there is one which is professedly taken from the Apostolic Constitutions (Acts xx. 35), to which pseudapostolic work an extreme antiquity was therefore assigned in Euthalius' mind. But Zahn points out that the quotation in question does not appear in the first form of the Constitutions, the Syriac Didascalia, which belongs to the third century, and that the Constitutions in their later form can hardly have existed as early as 370 and may be later than 400 A.D. Zahn suggests that a later hand should be credited with this quotation; but this is quite unnecessary; the difficulty only arises from a wrong chronological idea about Euthalius.

A further consideration of some weight is to be found in the fact that Euthalius speaks of Eusebius in a way which implies that he had been some time dead and had already acquired a literary canonisation. At the close of the Pauline prologue he imagines an objector who refuses to believe the details of Paul's second captivity on the ground that there is nothing of the kind mentioned in S. Luke. And the reply is that we should, on such a point, receive the testimony of Eusebius the Chronographer, and of his History. For it is those who follow the teaching of the Fathers and accept their traditions who will attain unto eternal life. The idea of replying to such objections comes from Euseb. *H. E.* ii. 22, but the manner of making the reply in which such deference is paid to the opinion of Eusebius, who is styled the Chronographer (which can hardly be a contemporary title), shews that Euthalius is writing after the death of Eusebius, and probably some time after. Now Eusebius died in 340. It would seem, therefore, a very unlikely supposition to assign Euthalius, with Prof. Robinson, to some date between 330—350 A.D.